D0445182

The Scarecrows of Saint-Emmanuel

The Scarecrows of Saint-Emmanuel

André Major

Translated by Sheila Fischman

McClelland and Stewart

Originally published as *L'épouvantail*
©1974 by Editions du Jour

The Scarecrows of Saint-Emmanuel
translated by Sheila Fischman
©1977 by McClelland and Stewart Limited

The Canadian Publishers
McClelland and Stewart Limited
25 Hollinger Road, Toronto

Design: Michael van Elsen

ISBN: 0-7710-5471-8

Printed and bound in Canada

I am grateful to my colleague, Joyce Marshall,
a patient, tactful, enthusiastic editor who
encouraged and supported me in the long
search for *le mot juste*.

S. F.

Major, André, 1942-
The scarecrows of Saint-Emmanuel

Translation of L'épouvantail.
ISBN 0-7710-5471-8

I. Title.

PS8526.A46E613   C843'.5'4   C77-001180-2
PQ3919.2.M282E613

PART I

PART I

1

Leaning against the wall behind the bed, breathing through his mouth, which made him think of a squashed tomato when he touched it, he prodded the right arm that he couldn't move without feeling shooting pains all the way up to his shoulder, and repeated, "Assholes, couldn't even tell I'm left handed!" Alone with his blue vinyl bag in the bedroom – nearly empty except for the bed, the chest of drawers, and the varnished wooden chair that stood between the sink and the window with the heavy flowered curtain – he was still shivering, hands clasped between his thighs. He had awakened an hour earlier, curled up in a garbage can he'd had a lot of trouble getting out of, and it had been just as hard to find his way back to the Tourist Room, lost and freezing as he was, but even worse had been climbing the dark stairs, holding his breath for fear of running into the landlord in the state he was in. He had thrown himself onto the bed without undressing, without even washing his face.

He tried to roll a cigarette, but it looked more like a cigar. He couldn't do it with just one hand. The paper didn't stick properly. With the tip of his tongue he explored the salty, spongy hole in the thickest part of his gum. Forgetting to light his cigarette, he spread the contents of his suitcase between his legs: a half-eaten chocolate bar with nuts, a red-and-black checked wool shirt, two hunting knives, one with a bone handle, the other with a plain, black wood handle which would do the job since Nico hadn't returned his switch-blade after forcing him to throw it into the door, while Vic threatened him with a revolver pointed at his stomach. He spread his left hand, closed it again, moving the fingers. "Not so bad," he thought, then aimed at the door, keeping his right eye open because the left one had disappeared under the swollen eyelid when Frenchy sunk his fist in it, an attack he had provoked by daring to ask, slumped down in Gigi's armchair: "You clean your teeth with shoe polish?" He'd said it without thinking, just for the hell of it, because he'd had enough of watching Frenchy circle the chair, displaying the rotten teeth in his big, laughing face. "That's for Marlene," Frenchy had said, and his fist closed Momo's eye. "And that's for the tax, you fucking hick!" This blow had cracked his knuckles, but he leaped to his feet, was stopped short by Vic's knee in his belly; then he stepped back, out of breath, before tumbling onto the edge of the bed, his right arm twisted behind his back while they punched him in the ribs, as he shouted, "My arm, my arm!" which made Frenchy laugh as he went on twisting the arm; then he had felt as limp as a rag, barely able to see Nico on the other side of the bed, tapping the ash from his cigarillo with the tip of his little finger: "Okay boys, cut it out." Frenchy, disappointed, asked, "Already? What do we do with him?" Nico shrugged. "Into the garbage can, boss?" Frenchy suggested. And Nico burst out laughing: "Takes a peasoup to come up with that!" He had felt hot all of a sudden, then nothing more until he came to, curled up in a ball at the bottom of an enormous, luckily odourless garbage can, so cold his fingers were numb, with the blood coagulated between his lips and in the stubble of his beard. Luckily, when he left the alley he found himself on Sainte-Catherine Street, the only one he knew, and from there he dragged himself to the Tourist Room.

He aimed at the door. The blade spun around once too

often, struck the hard wood and bounced off near the sink, just like when Nico had held the knife out to him after pushing the button – the dry click, familiar though it was, had chilled him – but he had taken the knife by the blade, expecting some dirty trick, while Nico, his low foreign voice chewing the words, spoke as though he were a schoolboy: "We're gonna play a game. Try and stick it in there. Just to see. In the door, get it? Don't miss, cause Vic won't." Vic, unsmiling, barely shifted his eyes; Momo even wondered if he were paralysed as he sat there on the edge of the bed, the revolver resting in the palm of his hand like some precious object. He heard Frenchy blowing in his hand, apparently looking forward to what would happen if he took the risk of not respecting the rules of the game. He sniffed, swallowing a mouthful of viscous liquid, a mixture of blood and saliva. Then his arm dropped to the side of his thigh while the knife rebounded close to Nico, who laughed heartily: "Looks like you lost your touch. How'd that happen?" Before he had time to answer, Frenchy pushed him into the chair where he had to sit, staring at the cigarillo Nico had just relit in the flame of a tiny lighter that operated without the slightest sound, as though the flame had burst out of its own accord when the tobacco approached. "I don't get it," he said, "a guy from the country comes to town to make trouble. You scared Gigi. That makes me sick...Not to mention what you done to Marlene." The other two didn't move. "It makes me sick, I can't tell you how much, Boulanger." And stubborn as ever, though it was useless to protest, Momo corrected him: "Baker. My name's Mo Baker." Blood poured from his mouth and he tried to swallow it. "When you get out of here," Nico replied, his thin lips curled like the mouth of a fish, "you ain't gonna know if your name's Baker or what." Frenchy laughed, slapping his hands. Nico added, "You got a good punch comin' to you after what you done, don't you think? After that I don't think you'd be dumb enough to try it again." He blew out some smoke, eyes creased, saying as though nothing had

9

happened: "Go get some exercise to get in shape, boys, but don't break his legs, okay? This little boy's gotta go back home," then Momo bent down, very stiff, to pick up the knife, while Frenchy walked around the armchair, as though wondering where to start, his smile revealing half-rotten teeth; but his smile disappeared when Momo, wanting to put an end to it, asked him if he cleaned his teeth with shoe polish.

And now he was staring at the blade, its rather thick tip, not yet sharpened, seeming to spear the drain-pipe, thinking: "I missed twice in a row – can't be," and he pulled the bone-handled dagger out of its leather case, sniffing at its odour, an old smell that had always moved him, "a female smell," then he weighed the still-oily blade in his hand, wiped it on the bedspread, and took aim at shoulder height. The shock as it hit the door made him sigh – the blade had gone in deep, without even quivering, and perfectly straight. "That's a nice one, Mo," he said, examining his left hand. He put one foot on the floor but immediately put it back on the bed. The match cracked, leaving a long brownish streak on the yellowing beige wall. The first puff tasted of sulphur. He spat on the floor, suddenly craving french fries, his hand against his painfully throbbing eye, and he remembered the brown paper bag stained with oil and vinegar on the bedside table in Gigi's room; and the moment he spotted it, he'd remembered that Sunday morning after Mass, in the cornfield...He had come to town the previous night, at dark, with just enough time to locate a cheap room and find his way around streets that were broad and dark as prison corridors. Luckily he had her address on the envelope she'd sent to Phonse. When he got to the house he'd wandered from one floor to the next until he found door number 9. He just had to slide the blade of a pocket knife into the crack and the latch yielded. He turned the handle slowly and the heavy odour of sleep, with another underlying odour that he knew well, gripped him, froze him to the spot. He could hear his heart beating very fast. He turned on the light with the back of his hand. A long sigh responded to the flood of light in the room, completely silent now that he had grown accustomed to the ticking of the alarm clock, no bigger than an orange, that stood under the lamp-shade. And he looked, fascinated, at the round arm, bent and freckled, the sole of the foot emerging from the sheet, crumpled as though something – a blade of grass or a sunbeam – had tickled it, and the pillow, so white under the shower of red hair.

He closed the door behind him, gently, and she sighed. He raised his arm, then lowered it: the blade pierced the varnished wood of the headboard. The disarticulated body stiffened before it turned over, tangled with the sheet, numb from being motionless too long; and her eyes, empty because they were grey, stared at him without seeing him, just holes in the mask of black eyeliner that made her face look as white as the pillow-case. The handle of the knife had stopped quivering above her raccoon's face. Her muffled voice, coming from her belly: "Scaring me like that..." He leaned against the door, face darkened by several days' growth of beard, parka open over a dirty red turtleneck sweater, and stared at her, motionless and unsmiling, melting snow pouring down his head. "Momo, if I'd'a known..." But he wasn't listening – the smell of french fries, an old, insinuating odour, had been stronger than the smells of sleep and sex that Sunday in the cornfield, not far from the restaurant with its smell of frying, and now it was coming from a greasy, crumpled paper bag next to the alarm clock. "Come down off your cloud when I talk to you, Momo." He answered, "My name's Baker." And she, in a tired voice, "Listen here, Momo..." He moved towards the bed with a sort of smile, very slowly, like a sleepwalker almost, head bent to the right, apparently drawn by the pink nipple in its narrow confine, high on the breast that resembled a half grapefruit when she sat up that way, he thought, and he sat on the edge of the bed, his hand on the warm white ankle. "That hurts," and she tried to move her foot. "I told

11

you to call me Baker, okay?" For that was the name with which he had been baptised, not because he wanted it, from the day when Kravenchuk, the Polack as they called him – though he was actually Ukrainian – had called him into the sawmill to sign him on. Old man Kravenchuk had trouble saying his name, stumbling over the second syllable so that it came out "Boulger," and he preferred – he was more comfortable in English than in French – to call him Baker. And, as though he had only been waiting for this new baptism, Momo had renounced his patronym and changed his style, becoming more sure of himself, almost arrogant, but people didn't seem to believe him, and he was obliged to lose his temper in order to persuade Gigi to drop her old, bad habit of calling him by the name he was born with. His clenched fingers squeezed her so hard she grimaced, stifling her urge to cry out. "Are you crazy?" He kept squeezing, looking down obstinately. She bit her lip. He released his grip. "Don't touch!" he said, in a voice no louder than if he were asking for a glass of water. He had seen her reach out towards the knife. "You're going to hurt yourself with that, Reddy." She was sitting up, her hair spread out around her head, speaking peevishly through the veil of thick curls that insulated her in a way, sheltered her from Momo's fixed and sombre stare. "My name's Gigi." He smiled to himself, his hand gliding down her leg to the firm round calf. She didn't shudder, only stiffened her leg at his caress. "How'd you manage to get in here?" No longer smiling, he seemed to be concentrating so hard that a wrinkle appeared between his bushy eyebrows, drawing them together. She placed the flat of her hand on his forehead, repeating: "I asked you something, Momo." It was as though he were biting something and couldn't unclench his teeth. Her hand was cool, he felt it running along his cheek, against his neck, like water; even her voice was softer: "I was just thinking about you yesterday. Funny coincidence, ain't it?" He was thinking of nothing at all, his hand squeezing her calf, the fingers sunk in the flesh, warm and tender under skin that

12

was smooth, a little bit prickly, wondering: "It was so long, two years nearly, I don't know how I took it." If only she had kept quiet, simply content to be there, in her own flesh, hadn't tried to delude him into thinking certain things: "I was waiting for you, Momo. I told myself you'd turn up some day. Take me back. I miss being back home so much." His hand squeezed her thigh, a kind of nervous contraction, while he answered as coldly as he could: "You should'a stayed there, it would'a saved me a trip. You had enough of the big city?" She sighed, reassured, almost certain she had tamed her "big wolf," telling him: "It hasn't been fun all the time – for you, I mean," and as he didn't answer she added: "We'll go home if you want, just give me a minute to pack my stuff." No sooner said than she slipped out of the bed, piling onto the back of the armchair, helter-skelter, her thin slip that crackled like onion skin, her brassiere that barely covered half of her breasts and her panty-hose, asking without looking at him: "What's new at home? Did Papa tell you anything?" She stopped, her voice quavering, feeling him behind her. "What's got into you?" He dug his fingers into the fatty part of her shoulder. "You're in a hell of a hurry, Reddy. Come on, not so fast." And as his hand closed like a hook around her shoulder, he pushed her towards the bed; she fell on her back, legs apart, so surprised at his roughness she didn't try to protect herself or even move aside when he fell on top of her with his full weight. Sitting on her belly, holding her crossed wrists above her head, he covered her nose and mouth with the pillow. He was breathing hard, as though he were the one lacking air, indifferent to her nails scratching at the thin skin of his wrist. She pounded his lower back with her knees. He pressed harder on the pillow, then, for no reason, threw it behind him. And when she saw him grimacing a sort of smile, she swallowed as much air as she could, breathing in his spicy sweat with the impression, the certainty even, that everything had already happened and this was only a repetition of some forgotten event. Her breath

13

whistled in her nostrils: "You're outa your mind. You nearly smothered me." He was laughing; she too, but in another way, as though forcing herself to please him. He removed the knife from the headboard. The blade grazed her throat. It was cold and she didn't dare swallow. "Quit that, Momo." But he kept moving the blade along her skin. "I'll do anything you want, but take that goddamn knife offa me." And he, leaping at the chance: "Anything?" She nodded. He stood up to take aim and stuck the knife in the window frame, an inch away from the venetian blind. The wood broke with a cracking sound. She helped him take off his parka. "My turn now, eh Reddy?" His fingers were spread like a star over the tuft of hair, not as red as the hair on her head, brown rather, thick and curly and climbing very high on her belly. She turned around and his hand slipped over the round part of her thigh. He leaned over her bent leg, his nose against the sole of her foot, then on the swelling at the base of her big toe. She said in a muffled voice, her nose in the fold of her forearm, "Come on, Momo." He ran his rough cheek along her calf, her rather heavy thigh, then swung to the other side, his mouth against her belly. She played with his thick, still-wet hair. He moved forward, licking her belly; his tongue warmed her hardened nipple. His leg pressed against her pubis, his hands gripped her shoulders as though to raise the rest of her body to his height. Her head thrown back in the russet mass of her hair, she looked at the ceiling while he kneaded her breasts in the hollows of his icy hands. "Go on, Momo, go on." But he didn't move, thinking that other men would be copying each of his actions that very evening and she would be telling them all the same thing, in the same way. She bit the fleshy part of his hand. "Do something or get off me!" He was kneeling, his hands on his thighs. "Get up, we're going out." And when she turned her back as she got up, he whacked her buttocks. The reverberation of this caress excited him again, and he didn't understand why, just then, merely by thinking of the others before him and after

14

him, no, he couldn't understand, "What got into me, just standing there like that when I'd gone without for so long?"

He took a deep breath and leaned on his left hand to get up. Once he was on his feet he felt weak and instead of going to get the dagger stuck in the door, he held onto the cold sink where the cigarette had fallen and looked at his face in the mirror. It was fogged by his breath and he couldn't see how he looked. He thought "It's better this way, at least I'm not scaring myself," but that didn't stop the throbbing in his right arm. The water ran colder and colder; he soaked the towel and covered his face, breathing deep at the shock, laughing as he remembered crazy Marlene who ran around the room with her sucker hanging down between her legs, but he was annoyed with himself for having been so rough. With the towel wrapped around his head he walked unsteadily, thinking again of that Sunday in the cornfield when Gigi had started to tremble, clutching his shoulders, and he had only asked her to swear there would never be anybody else – why demand that when he had her under him and he was the first one, maybe the last if he went about it properly? She had closed her eyes and her legs shut like scissors, without swearing as he'd asked her to do, and she grimaced when he insisted that he wouldn't go on until she yielded, and then she finally swore, tears in her eyes, and he went in between her slippery muscles, thinking: "If only it could go on forever," because it was so good, even better than seeing an animal writhing in its own blood, prisoner of a knife as murderous as a trap. "You swore," he repeated, holding the towel on his head, "you didn't have the right to go away with the first guy that came along in a Triumph while I was in there behind bars on account of you." He suddenly felt hot and it was as though something were smashing at his legs. "Don't tell me I'm gonna puke up the supper I didn't even eat." He barely had time to throw himself onto the bed when the walls began to spin and pound against his temples.

15

2

When he woke up he didn't know where he was or what time it was, and he had even less idea what he was doing there with a damp towel behind his neck; he was sure of only one thing, that he hurt everywhere, that wherever he touched himself the pain increased, as though responsive to the slightest contact, his left eye particularly. As he stretched out he felt a burning sensation spread through his stomach, "that goddamn buckle," he said, unfastening his wide leather belt, but the burning was inside, deep, untouchable, and he blamed it on hunger too long unappeased. And now that he was walking in the late afternoon cold, already dark, with no wind or snow, he slowly came back to himself and everything regained its meaning, from the moment she had told him, furious, "Do something or get off me!" and he had whacked her buttocks for the first time in his life. While she got dressed he waited outside, blowing into his hands that were stiff with cold – he hadn't thought of buying a pair of gloves when he got out of jail even though it was December – his feet in their felt boots already frozen. The snow wasn't very deep, though, an inch or two, no more, but she was taking her time, redoing her make-up maybe, and it was dark between walls of buildings so high they made him feel as though he were back in prison. He went back inside the lobby and spread his hands over the radiator which gave off a warmth that was steady,

16

like breathing; they were barely warm when he heard footsteps on the terrazzo stairs and she came out, powdered, her lips purple, looking broad in a red coat that was too short, he thought, open-mouthed, finding it hard to recognize her with her rabbit-fur collar, the high tower of her hairdo held in place by some kind of artifice, he didn't know what. "You've changed," he said at last, but she just tossed her head before saying, "I come a long ways while you were away." He thought: just wait till I shut you up! while trying to seem free and easy, his arm under hers. "Where we gonna go to celebrate?" he asked, but she didn't seem to see what there was to celebrate. Her purple lips gleamed like oil when she smiled. "You aren't the same with all that paint on your face," and he slipped his hand into her coat pocket. "Where we going?" he insisted. She jerked her chin towards the west, ahead of them. "To the Paradise," she said finally. The wind blew across them, damp and penetrating, promising snow. He clenched his teeth for fear his dentures would chatter as they had the night he was locked up with the others, who'd laughed, and the more they laughed the more his dentures chattered – there was nothing to do, just clench his teeth without saying a word as he waited for it to pass. The snow was turning yellow in the light of the street lamps. The entire street was deserted – not like now, with workers running, hurrying home to shut themselves inside, safe. "They're lucky," he thought, "they got a good supper waiting for them, a woman..." while, he, shivering in his parka, was swimming against the current, like a salmon returning to its natal waters. It was useless for him to clench his teeth and his hand was no warmer in her coat pocket; he took it out and stuck it into his own pocket where it struck the cold knife, reassuring as a fetish – a rabbit's foot or grandma's religious medal. He took out his hand when he saw her look down as a couple left a restaurant, "She's ashamed of me, hanging onto her coat," and he looked straight ahead at the red light, its brilliance filtered by the snow, then when they turned left, onto Saint-Lau-

17

rent, he was dazzled by the blinking sign of the Paradise, big yellow letters lighting a dancer with reddish skin, her breasts half covered by her long black hair. He asked in a rather troubled voice: "Is that where you hang out?" implying "to earn your bread" but Gigi, acting on some reflex, was already unbuttoning her coat as she walked ahead of him, climbing the stairs without the slightest hesitation, as though she had always climbed them, then waved to the waiter, very erect in his black jacket, choked by a bow tie, who pointed to the cloak-room, quite unnecessarily as it happened, since Gigi had already gone there by herself. Momo couldn't take his eyes off the square head pierced by two minute slits in which two black marbles glistened – eyes without pupils – then suddenly a smile puffed out the waiter's freshly shaved cheeks that looked lacquered, he signalled them to follow and led them to the back of the room, "Not too near the band," Momo whispered so as not to seem like a complete outsider, but he was astonished to see the waiter's smile disappear as he weighed the thin ten-cent piece Momo had dropped into his outstretched hand.

As soon as he was seated – without waiting for Gigi to pull out her chair or helping her to do so – he put his hands on his knees, feeling he was being watched, perhaps because he was sitting too straight against the back of the chair; then he took a large package of tobacco out of the pocket of his blue drill trousers and rolled a cigarette, staring fixedly at Gigi's décolletage, more moved than he wanted to be by the dark hollow between the round breasts in the brassiere that didn't even conceal the swollen raspberries of pink blood that made points under the thin beige wool of her dress. "Ain't you scared you'll get pneumonia with your tits hanging out like that?" She shrugged shoulders that were rounder than before, he thought, although still spotted with freckles; and he wanted to rub them, knead them, thinking of the pleasure he felt when he squeezed a hare that was about to die but still warm and trembling. He was content to sniff her heavy, spicy perfume, thinking that she hadn't

18

used any when she was still Phonse's girl, a country girl with no ambition but to find a husband and live a quiet life with her family. And she had to end up with him, who worked two or three months a year at the sawmill, shut down now since old Kravenchuk went broke. He was sniffing at Gigi's perfume, wondering what he would say to her, when she began, abruptly: "You still got your old bad habits," impatient, irritated at his irrepressible need to sniff at everything around him, his way of seizing the essence of things to appropriate them for himself or reject them, you never knew exactly which. He didn't understand, but she erased it all with a wave of her hand, giving him a kick to signal that the waiter was there, standing some distance from their table. "Two rye and tonics," he ordered, caught off guard, never having drunk anything but beer and the *caribou* that made the rounds of Saint-Emmanuel thanks to his brother Calixa and Gros-Jos; those two drank enough of it to be accurately called "goddamn drunkards," a title the village women bestowed on all members of the opposite sex. Momo ran the tip of his tongue along the sticky edge of the cigarette paper. "How about asking me what I want for once?" she asked dryly, but he laughed softly, a little more sure of himself now, thinking: You ain't seen the end of it, just wait, but not really knowing what he had in mind for her, just realizing that he had to pay her back for a betrayal that had sent him behind bars for twenty months and how many days, dying of boredom, all by himself, wondering what she could be doing with her body while he was doing nothing but what he was ordered to do – eat in the refectory buzzing with strange voices, walk in the large walled courtyard under the surveillance of guards, armed as though they were at war, and then go back to the cell he shared with two other prisoners from whom he had been separated after two weeks, because he kept them awake with his mania for walking up and down, whistling, as though seclusion had freed him of any normal need for sleep. In the place where he spent the rest of his time there

19

wasn't enough room to walk about comfortably, and even though he offered money to the guard who patrolled the corridor he couldn't obtain even a simple pocket knife which, in any case, wouldn't have been much help to him since there was nothing to use as a target. So he had invented another way to pass the time: lying on his stomach, eyes closed, as soon as he returned from the obligatory walk, he would disappear into the cornfield, the cobs crackling like dry paper, and then she would come to join him and he undressed her, taking his time, caressing her whole body, sniffing at all the odorous places, voluntary prisoner of her thighs, and a burst of warmth rose up in him and he came when he pressed the swollen berry of her breast between his lips, exploding inside her like the first time, better even because there was no wind or rain or refusal to swear that she'd be faithful to him, nothing but her and the freshly-ironed smell of her Sunday blouse.

She was smoking too, the cigarette almost hidden behind her hand, her face turned three-quarters to the band which was playing soft, languourous tunes, not altogether melancholy, just a little slow perhaps, as though the evening were getting off to a late start and the musicians were still warming up. A tall blonde came over to their table, her long silky pink dress shot through with phosphorescence and making a rustling sound; she smiled, saying rather mechanically: "How's things, Gigi?" and she, staring fixedly at the band leader, answered between her teeth: "You could'a picked a better time for a visit," and he wondered why. He spoke to Gigi, annoyed: "Who's the chick with all the paint?" Far from being offended, the tall blonde gave him a smile that showed all her teeth, so white and lustrous he thought they must come from the dentist, and without waiting for Gigi to decide to open her mouth, she said, "Marlene, good-looking." Momo kept sniffing: there were too many perfumes in the air, so spicy, so insistent that even the insinuating odour of cedar or sex would be dispersed, he thought, as Gigi got up and excused herself: "I'm going to the bathroom," and

Momo watched her as she walked away, trying to spit out a shred of tobacco stuck between his teeth, indifferent to Marlene who was now leaning against the back of the chair, still smiling: "You're kind'a cold, lover boy," then she pulled out the chair and sat down, thrusting her bosom towards the table. "I'll just stay and keep you company a minute because I already got two customers," pointing to two shaven heads, men in their late forties, who seemed to be telling a good one to judge by the laughter that contorted their faces. "You like her type?" Marlene asked, her eyes moist, and he felt something brush against his knee, not insistently, just a touch on the inside of his thigh. He blew smoke in her face. The hand was immediately withdrawn. He didn't even look at her but watched Gigi who was closing her purse as she came back to the table, distributing half-smiles to left and right as she passed, in response to greetings or calls noisily addressed to her, with no concern for the man waiting for her at the table. Momo was boiling, his cigarette dangling from his lips as though it were broken. "Who were you phoning?" he asked, infuriated at the kind of familiarity all around him which made him think that no matter what he did he would always be a stranger in this Paradise, so different from the Hôtel du Nord where, aside from big Jérôme's wife, Emérence, no woman from the village would ever set foot except to drag her husband home. But in such a short time, a little more than a year, he thought, she had learned how to swim in it like a queen surrounded by her court, a servant of the flesh borne on the wave of favours she had the magical gift of dispensing, rather absentmindedly. She shrugged as she sat down, but Momo didn't let her go, as though Marlene weren't even there: "So you'll never change, eh, two-faced?" To which Marlene, looking annoyed, replied placatingly: "You're a bad boy, lover. Some guys'd do anything to be in your shoes tonight." He laughed derisively, finding her so funny that he couldn't express his deepest thoughts – although his laughter did finally end: "You got

21

a hell of a swelled head if you think Reddy's gonna drop me," and stuck his index finger between her ribs, forcing her to mutter furiously: "Sure, Momo, sure," a grimace on her face, while Marlene, suddenly wondering if it was a joke, looked at each of them in turn, unable to leave them, repeating: "Okay, gotta go now. These two're getting worked up." And she disappeared among the tables, her haunches swaying with a sort of forced nonchalance. She was no sooner seated than she leaped up, waving her arms, letting out a shout of surprise, and the customer who had put his hand on her chair before she sat down was flushed with laughter. Momo barely smiled, then turned to Gigi: "Your work must be backbreaking. All those people don't leave you much free time, eh?" She put out her cigarette in the ashtray. The orchestra was silent; the only sounds were the clinking of glasses, sudden outbursts of voices, chairs scraping against the floor; then the curtain opened to reveal a large circle of light that was neither blue nor green, almost turquoise and in the middle of it stood a black-suited man with greying temples whom Momo took for a fifties-style singer, strange kind of singer, he thought, who instead of singing shouted: "And now, Mesdames-zay-Messieurs, the hit of the year, our world-famous star from Mexico City, the beautiful Lola in her famous dance number, the Featherless Bird. Mesdames-zay-Messieurs, Lola!" A low bow before disappearing at the same time as the lighting, while applause burst out from every corner of the room. Gigi hadn't turned towards the stage but stared at her untouched drink in which the ice cube had just finished melting. Momo wondered why the drummer was bending over to tap on his gilded disc, as though seized by a stomach cramp while trying to summon the distant Lola. Then nothing. Fits of coughing, throat clearing, and Gigi chewing at her thumb-nail. "You look like you ain't eaten for a week," he whispered, immediately distracted by the appearance of a greenish spot that moved across the stage looking for Lola, who came on suddenly with no announce-

22

ment but shouts of "Olé! Olé!" loudly acclaimed and sustained by a burst of music. It gave him shivers, he couldn't turn away from Lola, strutting about on her high silver heels to the rhythm of a chacha, a multi-coloured feather between her buttocks waving like a plume. She kicked one leg forward, then the other – Momo thought it was to toss off the sandals held to her feet by two thin crossed straps, and he sniffed, a little troubled by her trembling belly, the long muscle of her brown thigh, losing sight of her hands that were busy unhooking her black sequinned brassiere, so lacy the skin showed through. The music was drawn out into a searing lament, as though it pained the dancer to reveal her body to this curious audience, come there expressly to satiate themselves, the high point of the evening, he thought, then total silence; he even forgot the cigarette he was holding as he stared at the smooth bare heel, such a soft pink it made you want to take a bite, for she had turned her back to the crowd now, obviously a trick to make the impatient members of the audience yearn even more, to prepare a surprise that would be even more exciting than they had been trying to imagine for so long. Only the guitar accompanied the ritual of the hands searching for the hooks, then freeing her breasts of their fragile sparkling covering, which she whirled above her head before turning around, barely a half-turn to show her breasts in profile as they swayed to the rhythm of the music. Momo didn't return Marlene's wink, but Gigi took advantage of his distraction to get up, not fast enough, however, to escape the hand that clutched at her, forcing her back into the chair. "Sit down, Reddy, and stay still." Her wrist was numb in Momo's grip; he glanced at her quickly for fear of missing the rest of the performance, Lola tracing large Ss with the feather that burst out from between her buttocks, plucking it out with one movement and brandishing it like a trophy, the very symbol of her power over her breathless audience, groups of men whose hands rose to try to catch the feather; but it fluttered till someone caught it and put it

23

in safe-keeping, to a murmur of disappointment. And Lola, radiant, her eyes misty – Momo had the impression that she saw no one, that she was dreaming of her Mexican fiancé, in jail somewhere, and only agreed to show herself like that to earn enough money to get him out – yes, radiant, thinking of her Mexican, she was now threatening to lower her thin, black G-string covered with silver sequins, and her long brown hands with their scarlet nails, sharp as knife points, caressed her thighs as someone whistled and one customer, his nerves frayed, shouted hoarsely: "Take it off, what're you waiting for, Lola?" Momo released Gigi's wrist, fascinated by the slow movement of hands on thighs, by fingernails stuck into flesh, like large drops of blood, amazed as he saw a tuft of black hair emerge from the G-string, now rolled down very low, not noticing Gigi's mocking smile as she said: "As though you never saw pussy before." He made a nervous gesture, pinched the tender, fleshy part of her arm, "cheap meat," he thought, adding out loud, "Will you shut the hell up?" She tried to free her arm. "That hurts, you bully." But he dug his fingers deeper into the soft flesh, his teeth clenched, furious to be torn away from Lola who was still immolating herself for love of her Mexican: "Right now, Reddy, you're gonna clean the crap out of your ears and tell me who you were talking to on the phone when you went to the can." Her mouth closed like an oyster on the defensive, Gigi stared around the room at the waiter who had seated them, who now had his hands in his pockets adding up his tips, as indifferent as though she were alone, as though Momo's presence was accidental and inconsequential, while Momo went on with his interrogation: "I'd tell the truth if I was you; you know me, eh? I can put up with a hell of a lot, but when I get mad it ain't pretty." His bony fingers were paralysing her arm. "If you think I'm scared..." He laughed soundlessly, his face impassive, just a laugh from his throat: "Something's bugging me. I wanta know his name. You never know, maybe the two of us could get together sometime, you know?" The crowd gave Lola an ovation and she lingered on the stage, throwing kisses left and right as the heavy velvet curtain closed on her; now the sound in the Paradise was a vague murmur of voices, the scraping of chairs, waiters rushing to serve thirsty customers. Momo must have loosened his grip at the arrival of the waiter who stood head down, eyes half shut, like a priest behind the grille of his confessional, waiting for him to order: "Same again. Two rye and tonic," he said, powerless to restrain Gigi who had moved her chair so she was facing him: "Why couldn't you of stayed down there? Leave me in peace..." He laughed unpleasantly, the cigarette hanging from his lips, answering without thinking, telling her just what was on his mind: "That's what you call peace? I get the feeling you spend most of your time changing the sheets." She tapped her cigarette, still staring at him, her grey eyes grown very dark in the false light, the penumbra that smelled of duplicity, an equivocal kind of collusion. Then, spitting out her words with a conviction that had something final and irrevocable about it: "You had to come, didn't you? Like as if I'd called you, eh? Things were going too good for me. It couldn't last." But the waiter had come back, his napkin folded over his arm, and he put their drinks on the table with an air of disdain which the fifteen-cent tip conceded by Momo justified for a second time. He was content to sigh as he left them, as promptly as a spring unwinding. She didn't dare touch her drink, perhaps because she owed it to the person she was beginning to attack again, in the same arrogant voice: "Where's it gonna get us if we start up again, will you tell me? We'll just be at each other's throats and I'm not interested. I've had it up to here and I wanta live my own life now." And he, taking time to gulp down half his rye, replied calmly: "Ah, so your pimp lets you go out on your own, eh?" She seemed not to understand, still tapping her cigarette, which she hadn't had a chance to smoke and which was burning away. "What pimp? Say something I can understand." She spoke so loud that Marlene and her two customers turned around.

25

"Don't yell," Momo said, uncomfortable, "people're looking at us. I just said, your pimp leaves you alone, eh?" She
put out the cigarette and grabbed her purse, as though getting ready to leave him there: "I just got one thing to tell
you, Momo Boulanger..." She was interrupted by the kick
he gave her under the table and bent over to rub her leg,
ignoring the looks her shout was attracting. He, expressionless: "My name is Mo Baker." Then, still gritting his teeth:
"You got a short memory and that ain't good." She closed
her fists: "Son of a bitch!" Not another word; he raised his
glass: "My health," then downed the rest of his rye so fast
that he belched several times, acting like a boor, she realized, so he would seem to be above conventions and even
the most elementary respect for another person; it was also
his way of letting her know he had no reason to feel embarrassed in the company of an old acquaintance, so intimate
that after long months of separation he still associated her
with his own existence. He didn't see the three men come
in. A space cleared around them, an imperceptible murmur
of fearful admiration rising around them. All three were
young, particularly the tallest whom the other two seemed
to be escorting. He was long and thin like a mannequin,
wearing a very stylish suit, a wide red necktie on a discreet
pale blue shirt that showed off his tan, like a young star so
sure of himself he could afford a haughty expression, even
afford to move without a care for the rest of humanity in his
path. He stopped in the middle of the room, halfway
between the lobby and the corner where Momo, at his
table, was wondering who Gigi's nervous smile was meant
for. And when he turned around, Gigi jumped up and wove
between the tables without giving him time to figure out
what was going on. He knocked his chair over in his haste
to get up, and stood in total silence in front of Nico, hands
in his jacket pockets, and said to him: "Give me some air!"
But already the waiter, flexing his shoulders, had come up
with his springy step, asking: "Trouble, boss?" Momo
found it hard to distinguish the four men, who formed a

semi-circle around him, but looked over their heads for Gigi as they stood there motionless, determined to block his way. He felt a hand on his shoulder and heard Marlene telling him in a low, pleading tone like a mother trying to calm a rambunctious child: "Keep still, good looking. Come on, you haven't even finished your drink." He felt vaguely that it would be better if he let himself be led back to his table.

3

He had stopped looking over the tops of the houses that
formed an endless wall on either side of the street; there was
nothing more to see up there now that night had fallen like
a canopy, closing him completely inside a kind of deserted
labyrinth where no one would turn around as he went by,
astonished or smiling at his black eye and swollen lips; he
walked slowly, dragging his feet, a stiffness in the muscles of
his calves, and for the moment nothing could stop him, not
even the uselessness of his wandering, even though it
seemed absurd to be walking like that, just for the sake of
walking, as though the fabulous sum of his steps would finally lead him somewhere, or at the very least make him dis-
cover some goal to be reached, while the one really
important thing to do was drink some hot coffee and take
some time to rest and get warm. And he listened to the gurgling of his empty stomach, deprived of food since the previous night, when Marlene had dragged him off to her
place on the pretext of giving him some vegetable soup and
grilled-cheese sandwiches which she claimed she made better than the restaurant, and he had been foolish enough, or
rather drunk enough, to snap at the bait; and instead of the
smell of soup he'd had to put up with the church smell that
always made him gag. As soon as they were inside her
apartment she lit a stick of incense in a block of wood that
occupied the place of honour on a chest of drawers painted

28

a blue so transparent the veins and knots showed through, marbling the smooth surface; he leaned against it after pushing back the thin white curtains so he could watch the snow fall on the dark glistening street, all the while forcing himself to belch, to get rid of the bubble that was nauseating him, but without success. On the contrary, the incense made him feel worse. He turned his back to Marlene, who was sprawling against the cushions spread across the wide, almost square bed, humming "l'Important c'est la rose" while he repeated, as though to put an end to his disgust: "That stuff makes me sick, goddamnit, it really makes me puke!" She looked at him without understanding: "Come on, stop thinking about it." He turned around, furious, pointing to the smoking incense. She pouted, then said in a sullen voice: "All you have to do is put it out." He crushed the burning stick between his fingers, surprised to feel nothing but a slight sensation of warmth, then walked heavily over to the bed and dropped onto it, arms crossed behind his neck, eyes wide open, for as soon as he lowered his eyelids the bed began to spin, taking him with it. He noticed, close to his knee, Marlene's long bony white foot, and he thought that he wouldn't be able to sniff it or lick it with the tip of his tongue. Only his chest was moving, swelling and deflating the red sweater, soaked under the arms, and she slipped a damp hand under it, just cold enough to cool his chest. "You're so hot it's terrible," she said, undoing his wide black leather belt. She rubbed him, as far as his sex. He was stiff, shaken by sudden uncontrollable trembling, and he spoke to keep his mind clear: "It's the tall guy with the red tie, isn't it?" A velvet ring was warming his sex, which had risen up between the folds of his trousers. His question remained suspended there between his lips and the warm breath, like the steam from boiling water, which caressed him slowly and more gently than Reddy had ever done, even when everything was going well between them. There were long pulsations in his sex. He felt as though he were melting in the warmth of her mouth, while hoping it

29

would go on forever, like the first time he had felt Reddy's slippery muscles pressing against his penis that Sunday noon in the cornfield. And his deep breathing filled the whole room, barely lit by the electric light over the bed, and Reddy, open-mouthed under him, shook her head even as she was swallowing him in the slippery slopes of her thighs. His desire had been building up for several days and now it came gushing out in long continuous spurts, and he stopped clenching his teeth. They were chattering in his mouth. He couldn't understand the enormous disproportion between his pleasure and the slight attraction he felt for the tall blonde bony woman coiled between his legs, out of breath, hands trembling on his thighs, postponing the satisfaction of her own desire which had been intensified by the pleasure she had just dispensed. He dared not look at her as long as her face was disturbed by the simple appetite which, he thought, let her earn her living without too much disgust, probably more easily than Reddy. When he held his hand out to her a sort of sudden fear made her move away from him and leap out of the bed, tangled in her long pink dress. He thought he'd been treated like any other client recruited at the end of a show whose goal was not only to make the audience drink but to instil in them a violent need for flesh that would be satisfied later by some eager servant, the reason, in fact, why Marlene, Reddy and the others like them sat at their tables, wearing low-cut dresses, with the Paradise regulars. He got up, ears still buzzing, wondering what she was doing shut up in the bathroom. He pushed the door open and then, paralyzed by shock, he saw her sitting on the white bowl, her head thrown back, stark naked and squeezing in her hands nothing less than a male penis, scarcely different from his own; a burst of heat rose to his head and he kicked the door, slamming it into the radiator. She looked so lost he wouldn't have believed her capable of diving under his arm to disappear towards the door. He shouted: "Wait a minute, you fuckin' queer!" furious that he held in his hands only a curly blonde wig, a light and ridiculous head-covering without which Marlene was forced to admit that she was only a young man with short, dark-brown hair, defenceless now, fit only for flight – and for pleasure when she managed to find a client indifferent enough to the sex of the person bestowing it on him. Marlene had picked up the bedspread on her way and was running towards the door; just as she was about to open it Momo threw his knife into the wood. She fell to the floor, her face in her hands, her back curved, the spine projecting under too-white skin. Momo kicked her in the ribs, provoking a strangely harsh rattling sound but not the slightest cry, as though she felt obliged not to alarm the neighbours; he had seen her face turned towards him, more astonished than sad, a pink colour that contrasted with the whiteness of the back and shoulders. He struck out in every direction, until finally she began to choke from the effort of crying and trying to hold her breath. "Don't bawl, crazy, your trouble's just starting." Curled into a ball, hands between her thighs, Marlene accepted his blows, biting her lips. "It's kind'a late to be shutting the barn door now!" Momo shouted. She blushed with shame because it was true that her large ears stuck out without the wig and even though she lay there out of breath, this too direct allusion to what she considered an infirmity wounded her more than the blows. She looked at the floor as she got up, forced by the pressure Momo was applying to her twisted arm. Then a vicious slap flung her onto the bed, deaf in one ear, barely hearing Momo's laughter; he was almost happy, it seemed, to see her so weak and to be able to say with his air of male superiority: "This is the first time I ever seen a female with a handle. You wouldn't be so bad if you didn't have that sucker between your legs. But will you tell me how come you ain't got a single goddamn hair on you down there? Do you shave it all off twice a day?" She was sniffling, curled up like a snail, one hand protecting her burning ear, as though she were crushed by Momo's contempt, someone she hadn't even known three hours earlier; now he was

31

wringing all the tears from her body, just as he might have made her gasp with pleasure if he'd been someone else. But he didn't even allow himself to consider this possibility as he stood at the foot of the bed, neither tall nor stocky, rather nervous, his complexion as dark as the maroon sweater that stuck to his chest where, a little earlier, she had felt the crackling of fine muscular currents, and he seemed calm, soothed by his own violence, a gleam of mockery in his expression, as though he needed to avoid any form of tenderness and was struggling also, no doubt, against the discomfort caused by her passive, proffered nudity. It wasn't so much the transvestite whom he blamed as the half-man who had dared not only to pass for a female but to affront without scruples (so he thought) someone of his own sex; and now that his body had been unmasked he seemed to be innocently assuming the role of victim. Momo crossed his arms, avoided looking at her – or him – and insisted on being told everything about what was still a mystery to him: "What'd you call yourself before you decided to be a girl?" She said nothing for fear of adding to her humiliation a meekness that would have justified the contempt which still kept him near her, but her prolonged silence might provoke a new avalanche of blows, and she pretended to be offended: "That isn't funny." She said it without protecting herself from the hand which struck at her thigh, just closed her eyes and accepted the burning pain. He struck her mechanically, furiously, as though to avenge himself for the pain he felt with every blow: "God-damn pile of bones!" And then he got up onto the dresser, after sweeping everything off the top – the wooden block with its stick of incense, the box of kleenex, the teddy bear with one ear missing and the photograph album – and rolled himself a cigarette, sighing profoundly like a labourer taking a couple of minutes' rest, but his hands trembled so much that he had to take out a new paper and start again, a painstaking operation; she took advantage of it to curl up under the thick yellow blanket that scratched her skin, distracting her from the growing pain pounding between her ribs whenever she breathed even a little deeply. He sniffed at each puff of smoke that came out of his nostrils, as though he wanted to swallow it at the very moment he was expelling it. She was so tired that everything made her feel cold inside, and when he shouted: "Ain't you got nothing to say, baby?" she barely stirred, eyes burning, waiting for his blows, even provoking them to get it over, make him feel disgust at his own violence: "You think you're pretty smart but I know some people that'll make you pay through the nose." She wanted to sound tough, but she sniffled as she spoke. Momo didn't look up from his wet felt boots, from his leg which he swung back and forth, as he said in a low voice, almost to himself, after much apparent reflection: "You know, if they find a queer like you soaking in his own blood there ain't nobody's gonna be surprised." This time Marlene got up, but he jumped to the floor and grabbed her. "Can't I even put some clothes on my back?" she asked, and he laughed. "If I was you it isn't my back I'd be hiding." She shrugged as she went over to the wardrobe and pulled a heavy yellow woollen dressing-gown off a hanger, slipping it on quickly, as though she were about to open the door to an unknown visitor. "You're ashamed of your little sucker," Momo said. But she sat down on the bed, legs crossed, making no reply, holding an unlit cigarette. "What does that big slob do at the Paradise?"

"He's the boss."

He smiled, embarrassed to see her suddenly so obliging, not passive like before. "What does he live on?"

"Same as everybody else."

Momo moved his hand forward to warn her that he wasn't laughing, and she took refuge in the middle of the bed. "Reddy works for him, eh?" She sighed. "They're together, aren't they?" She shrugged, added: "Depends. Sometimes yes, sometimes no. Nico's got all the broads he wants." He burst out laughing: "Even women like you?"

33

She stuck out her tongue, not for long because his hand smashed into her teeth and he shouted, overcome with rage: "You got sharp teeth, eh?" His fist was deflected off her chin, struck her throat and made her choke. He was still shouting, revolted at the way she acted, like a scared dog: "At least you could pretend to be defending yourself, you stinking animal!" But Marlene was rubbing her throat as though a bone were stuck in it, ignoring her dressing-gown which was open on her belly and thighs. He stepped back, frightened at the pallor of her face. She was breathing with difficulty, jerkily, and he said without really laughing: "I'd eat you if I was inclined that way," and tossed a satin cushion in her face. "Go sleepy-bye baby," he added by way of farewell, then pulled his knife out of the door and picked up his parka which he had tossed to the foot of the bed when he came in. Marlene dug her fingers into the cushion, motionless, hardly daring to breathe.

His hand hurt. The cold wind went right through him, spread through his body. And gusts of powdery snow were turning the street, the houses, and the sky to white. He wandered around, bent over to escape the wind. He had crossed one street, not too sure where he was going, then a second, the one he called the big street – there he could see clearly – and the wind was at his back. He squeezed his knife in the palm of his hand.

4

His eyelids were flickering as they'd been the evening he
went to her place, not suspecting that they were waiting for
him and he'd pay dearly for his night with Marlene. The
bare bulb in the middle of the ceiling stung his eyes and he
had to cling, as he walked, to a rough wall as unpleasant to
touch as a blackboard, especially when your nails screeched
along it. He was covered with goose pimples. He had seen
number 7 on a door, no longer quite sure he was in the right
house, though he had recognized the façade by the spruce
tree spattered with luminous stars; then after a few steps he
remembered that the number on her door was 9. He was
there. He breathed deeply, as though to push aside the
insidious rise in his fear, yet unable to prevent himself from
thinking: I must'a been crazy to go in to her place when I
saw the door was open! He had just pushed it open and
stepped inside when it slammed behind him and an arm
came down across the back of his neck – a blow that had
shaken him so much that everything went black. He hadn't
had time to pull himself together when they made him
spin. Then his foot caught, he wasn't sure in what, impossible to know, and he was stretched out, his nose striking the
floor, but he stayed cool enough to think: My knife, my
knife; his hand already inside his pocket, grasping the cold
weapon, when the foot hit him in the stomach, "that was a
crazy idea, to go back there when I saw him coming," and

35

he rolled on the ground, choking, hands pressed against his stomach as though to contain the pain within as small a space as possible. They pulled him up by the hair, just long enough to empty his pockets. Without his knife, eyes wet, he fell to his knees, panting the way he did when he came out of the water, in front of Nico who had a second bulldog on his heels and looked as though he'd just carried off a good deal, still wearing the same red necktie, with a yellow shirt this time, thin red lips pinched together in a sort of smile. Frenchy had thrown him the knife and he was weighing it in his hand, still the same bully he'd been when he barred Momo's way at the Paradise, with one of his killers on either side and the zealous maître d' asking him: "Trouble, boss?" The memory infuriated Momo and suddenly, without thinking, he threw himself at Nico's legs, throwing him off balance, and fell on him with his full weight while Frenchy, standing nearby, mouth open, hands dangling, watched them fight; but Vic was just waiting for a chance to intervene, and when it came he kicked Momo in the face: when Momo shut his mouth again he bit on something hard and salty. Nico got up, out of breath, and fixed his hair, a forced smile breaking the feminine curve of his lips; then he moved his foot forward, brought it down on Momo's hand, spread out on the floor. When he shouted he spat out the broken tooth, but Nico kept on crushing the fingers of his right hand. He heard them crack. Nico moved his foot to play with the blood-stained tooth. Momo saw the black shoe, very shiny, push his tooth, bring it back, then finally try to stick it into the linoleum; he also saw his own hand, which was hurting so much he didn't dare move it, and the three pairs of wide-spread legs surrounding him, "all set to cut me up," he thought again, his back against the wall, breathing as silently as possible through his mouth; he'd spent a fair bit of time lying in a heap at their feet, unable to close his hand, blood in his mouth. He spat and Frenchy said: "Don't dirty up Gigi's room, you fuckin' pig!" Nico came between them, his honeyed voice saying,

"Don't yell at him. He already looks like shit." Frenchy sighed, "Bah!" All three laughed, then Nico said: "Stand him up on his feet, but careful you don't lose any of the pieces." Momo would have given anything to be able to punch him between the eyes, but Vic put his hands under his arms and he barely managed to stand up, still shaken by the kick that had cost him one of his few remaining teeth. And afterwards, once he was on his feet, what happened? He saw Frenchy walk around him, spit in his hands and rub them together, looking as though he wanted to chop down a tree that was blocking his view of the sun. Vic sat on the edge of the bed tossing a big revolver in the air, waiting for Nico to come over and return Momo's knife, saying: "Try throwing that, just to see. In the door...." And he picked up the knife by the blade, swallowed his salty saliva, sniffed several times before taking aim – and missed. But this evening he didn't feel like being taken the way he'd been that other time, to get the worst beating of his life, and wake up half frozen in the bottom of a garbage can. He wondered just when he'd passed out – when he was being carried out of Gigi's place on Frenchy's back or later, on the stairway, when Frenchy dropped him. He couldn't remember; one thing for sure, it had happened and it was a bad fifteen minutes he wouldn't forget. It was early now and Gigi must be still hanging around at the Paradise, having a drink or two before bringing her client home, probably sure he was on his way to Saint-Emmanuel, cursing her as he went. No light showed under her door. It was the right time to go in – a risk to be taken if she didn't come back alone. His dagger was in its place, in the case with the strap undone. The door handle turned in his hand but when he pushed it, nothing. He did what he'd done the first time, slipped the thinnest blade of his pocket knife into the slit, worked it for a moment between the wood and the steel tongue, and then he had it; but he stood there undecided, hands trembling. Someone was lumbering up the stairs: the footsteps came closer. He thought you could see to the very end of the corridor from the top of the stairs and he pushed the door with his knee. The room was dark; not even the bedside light was on. He closed the door behind him before tiptoeing to the bathroom where he jumped into the tub just as he heard a key unlocking the door. The wet soles of his shoes slid along the surface of the tub; luckily the shower curtain was opaque. Gigi had some joker with her who was laughing, for lack of anything better to do, he supposed, or perhaps out of shyness. He thought: "I can't move, you bastards, but I got a nice surprise for you," his head pressed against the cold tiles, hands flat against the wall to avoid slipping. Gigi sighed, already tired it seemed, while the man walked heavily, the floor creaking when he put one foot in front of the other, whistling as though he were back home after a good day at work, and Momo had to hold his breath when he walked into the bathroom. Water came pouring out of the tap. He stopped whistling. The door was almost completely closed. Momo clenched his teeth, unable to decide to act, just waiting for the water to stop splashing in the sink; then he moved his head a few inches, just enough to see that he was alone, a blind witness to the slightest rustle of clothing, the client chuckling as he wallowed in Gigi's flesh, no longer accessible to Momo; it was as though he understood now what he had come to the city to look for: the certainty that it was useless to go back; besides, he didn't know why he had needed this tangible proof that Gigi was excluded from his life for good now, a life so deserted and empty it seemed senseless just to go away, relieved of any further waiting; but he still couldn't close his eyes and laugh at the shame burning his cheeks as he listened to them moving like solitary wrestlers, she to earn her living, he to have what his wife was perhaps no longer able to give him: the surprise of a new body, never seen or touched before, at least by his eyes and hands. He wanted to slip down into the bathtub, run the water and float there like a dead fish delivered from its hunger and fear and desire, but something held him back, kept him standing on his aching legs, despite the cramp in his thigh, watching or rather listening for the harsh groan, proof positive of Gigi's fate. The bathroom smelled of soap, as the other man had washed himself before going to join her and obtain what he, Momo, had never had – light-hearted pleasure, the simple pleasure of a caress, and her laughter too; for she was laughing now – he wondered why; he should have moved farther, even at the risk of being seen, so he could watch the big man taking off his pants, staggering as one foot held up the edifice of his corpulence. All he could hear was Gigi, laughing as she said: "Sure can't see much of the family jewels under that belly!" He held his pants in his fist, his heavy breathing shaking the folds of his torso where all the muscles had been drowned for a good quarter of a century, Gigi thought as she watched him, still laughing, except when she said: "Bet you don't know where I come from: a hole in the woods called Saint-Emmanuel de l'Epouvante," which brought a reaction from the big man, who finally pulled up his pants: "Hey, that's funny. I got a brother, the oldest one, he's got a business down there. The Hôtel du Nord. Ever hear of it?"

"Sure."

"What's your old man's name?"

"Jolicoeur."

"You wouldn't be related to Phonse, would you?"

"That's my daddy."

"Hey, that's the best one I ever heard!" he exclaimed as he waddled over to the bed, almost falling onto it when he tripped, laughing uncontrollably; she laughed too, sitting with her legs dangling over the side of the bed. "How about that?" he said, "I just slept with Phonse's girl! Jeez, I almost feel like starting all over again!" But Gigi rolled over to escape the hand held out to her, and said: "Better save your strength if you're gonna spend the rest of the night at home." He resigned himself to buttoning his shirt, dreaming out loud: "How about that – I can't believe it – Phonse's girl! We used to drink together pretty often back in the old days, before he met your late mother; she was a

39

real nun, just between us, wouldn't even let him out. Poor old Phonse, shaking the rugs. Who'd'a thought I'd end up with his girl, right here in the city!" Momo clenched his teeth. She asked him, in her astonishing laughing voice: "So you must be related to big Jérôme?" He pulled up the narrow suspenders that made his shirt puff out and answered in the same tone: "Guess I am."

"You look a lot like him."

"Well – maybe I'm a little thinner, just a bit ..."

"Don't really show," Gigi replied, distant, turning the radio on so that Momo couldn't hear Gène: "I'm gonna go and make myself beautiful." His heavy footsteps warned Momo of his intrusion into the bathroom. Before he closed the door Gène turned around to ask: "Does Phonse know what you're doing with your time?" She replied, still fiddling with the dial of the radio: "He thinks I'm a salesgirl somewhere." Gène thought that was a good one: "Salesgirl? Well, I got to admit you sell some pretty fancy stuff," and then he shut the door, closing himself in with Momo; the radio couldn't be heard over the sound of running water.

Gigi was listening to the radio absentmindedly, looking between the slats of the venetian blind at the lightly falling snow and thinking: "There's gonna be more, it ain't over yet." She tied Gène's brown necktie, then untied it, wound it around her wrist, felt herself becoming angrily impatient – her old fear of winter, the dead season, the land white as far as you could see, the weighty silence of Saint-Emmanuel broken only by the steady creaking of the floor under the rocking chair or the dry crackling of wood in the stove – and to overcome her profound irritation she told herself, trying to convince herself, that her life wasn't as dull as it used to be, even if it didn't have any secrets for her anymore. And she'd never go back to live with her father. She touched the wood of the windowsill as though to assure herself of the complicity of fate. She slapped at her leg, impatient for Gène to leave, smiling at the thought that he was trying to make himself handsome. Then she could order something from the restaurant before her Friday night client arrived. She didn't feel like going out in the snow. She closed her dressing gown and went towards the bathroom. The door was open and she stopped, frozen, before Momo, barely recognizable with one eye invisible under the swollen lid, his lips blackened with dried blood, trying to smile at her. She held the folds of her dressing gown over her belly, the brown necktie still wound around her wrist. "Hi," he said, but she didn't react, too surprised to make any reply at all, staring first at the swelling that deformed his eyebrow, then behind him, as though she were expecting an accomplice to appear, big Gène perhaps. Only the shower curtain had been moved and was stretched out along the steel rod now. "Is he in there?"

"He's taking a nap," Momo answered.

She hesitated, not too sure whether she wanted to know any more: "I hope he isn't sleeping too sound." Momo closed the door as he answered, "Just enough so we can't hear him." She instinctively took a few steps backwards, and he smiled, tried to smile rather, with the corner of his mouth. "What'd you do all day?" she asked, one foot inside her pink slipper. Momo wiped his lip with a stained handkerchief. Then she put her other foot into her slipper, which was open toed like a sandal. He seemed to be drawn by the painted nails of her stubby toes, curved slightly towards the sole. "Who did that to you?" she asked, but he looked at her with one eye, black and sparkling in its almond-shaped cavity, "he's got an eye like a hawk," she thought, unable to control the trembling of her hands as she lit a cigarette, which he took from her mouth to have a puff. The filter tip was stained when he gave it back to her. He sniffed, sensitive to the odour which was not his but similar all the same, and which was permeating him. "Fucking pig!" She just had time to step back to avoid a blow that made him lose his footing, as though this unsuccessful gesture was the last effort he could make, after his long wait behind the shower

41

curtain and the settling of accounts between Gène and himself. He leaped onto her as she took refuge behind the bed, brandishing one of her high-heeled shoes. Before he had time to jump on her the heel struck his temple. She stood there dazed, seeming not to believe that this simple act had stunned him so that he had to lie down on the bed, his body streaming with sweat, breathing through his mouth. She came back quickly with a damp towel, which she put over his face. It was so cold it took his breath away. Then without opening his eyes, knowing she was kneeling close to him, he slipped his hand inside her dressing gown, then down her tense thigh, and caressed her as though this same avid hand had not tried just a minute earlier to strike the flesh which was the only thing in the world still left to him, and which he had thought he would possess forever, one stormy summer Sunday afternoon. Gigi must have shuddered because the skin on her thigh became prickly as though it were covered with minute bumps. He barely heard her say, with a hiccup or a sob: "I know you're fed up to the teeth with me, Momo, and it's all my fault, but what the hell do you want? That's how I am. I'm the wrong girl for you. We couldn't...You understand? You should get out of here fast. If the others come back all of a sudden, you know, it'll be a hell of a lot worse. Are you listening? I'm telling you this for your own good, I don't want nothing to happen to you," and as she spoke she was rubbing his shoulder, not knowing she was relieving the pain a little. He hadn't opened his eyes for fear that everything would be finished, this well-being, Gigi's repentance, and he repeated: "Don't cry, Reddy, it makes me sick. You aren't a little girl, come on..."

"I'm not crying, I'm suffering, I got the right to suffer for once in my life."

He turned his head and as he opened his eyes he noticed some money that had been slipped under the alarm clock. "Order in something to eat," he said. And she, sniffling like him, "Right away?"

"I'm starving. I don't know when was the last time I had anything to eat."

She got up, seeming to look for something: "You want Chinese food?" He replied, eyes closed, "I don't care, anything. And a large Export. You watch it, now...don't go calling any wrong number..."

"What kind'a dope do you think I am?"

And she pulled the phone off the hook.

5

They were sitting with their backs propped against the pillows, and she was watching him nibble at his chicken leg, breathing in his pungent odour, sweat so strong it stained his shirts, sheets and pillow-case. His lip stung, especially when he drank Coke from the bottle. She thought: "He's gonna let out a good belch any minute now." Almost immediately he confirmed her thought by rubbing his belly and letting out three belches in a row, beaming. "Remember that time you were drinking a Pepsi in front of the store one Sunday when there was a real strong wind?" She was asking him that: He just had to lower his eyes, not even closing them, and it was as though he could feel the grains of sand in his mouth again and the wind that smelled of rain. People were hurrying faster than usual, not stopping to chat on the lawn in front of the church. As soon as he came out he'd gone and bought a Pepsi which he drank slowly, leaning against one of the posts of the enormous gallery that made the general store even more impressive than the Town Hall with its four grey steps and no bannister. He was waiting for her, amazed that she was lingering so long after the "Ite missa est" marked the end of contemplation or simply of any effort to participate in a ceremony of which he had never understood a thing, except that it had been the inevitable beginning of every Sunday since he was old enough to talk and get around by himself. Then, in a dusty gust of wind, she came down the lane bordered with aspens and maples, her nose in the air, not looking at him, as though she hadn't seen him, as though she had not once, throughout the sermon, glanced his way, she and her pink-ribboned straw hat, pinching her Saint-don't-touch-me lips (his name for her), it was only for show because later, when he invited her to go for a walk, she didn't say no, but she didn't really say yes either; she just hesitated, saying her father would worry if she was late, but she followed him all the same, rather absently, a little against her will, as far as the gap in the fence around the cornfield on the outskirts of the village. She sat on the ground a few steps away from him, in spite of the darkening sky and the gusts of wind that stripped the tops from the ears of corn. Momo burst out laughing and some of the cola came pouring out his nostrils. She looked at him, frowning: "Your hat..." he said. The wind had blown it away, making it roll among the tall cornstalks like a hoop. He caught it and put it back on her head, then stood in front of her, one hand on her shoulder. She bent her head, her cheek pressed against his warm hand, neither one daring to move, to go farther or to undo what had already been done, there amid the dry rustling of corn bending in the wind. She put her hand on his thigh and he knelt between her naked legs.

"You didn't even move," she said. "You were waiting for me to make the first move. I never seen anybody as embarrassed as you."

"You were getting me worked up but you were scared, you kept saying, papa's gonna wonder what I'm doing."

"It was the first time."

"You're still trying to make me swallow that?"

"But I already told you!"

"You sure seemed to know your way around."

"Well, one of us had to do something. You kept on kissing me and kissing me. My mouth was bleeding."

"Well anyway, an ordinary girl wouldn't'a been in so much of a hurry."

"I swore it was the first time I done it. And if you don't believe me that's tough."

"Yeah, and you swore something else that wasn't true neither."

She jumped out of the bed, stepping on the cord of her dressing-gown: "That was crazy too, making me swear something when my mind was somewheres else. And you had the nerve to blame me afterwards. You men think all us women are just waiting around for you to tell us what to do. You can do whatever you want but a woman's supposed to sit and twiddle her thumbs and wait around for you."

"But you swore."

"Yeah, and you were too smart to swear nothing. You were too smart for that. There wasn't nothing to stop you doing whatever you felt like. If I'd'a known I sure wouldn't have swore nothing, I wouldn't even'a done what I did, especially when it started raining cats and dogs."

Momo laughed quietly, from the back of his throat, his teeth clenched, with the scent of dried weeds in his nose, then the smell of wet earth mixed with the salty smell of her damp skin, while he was swaying inside her – her plaintive, mocking laughter, the hard swollen gums of her nipples – and the smell of frying fat that the wind blew in their direction, giving them another kind of appetite. "We were so hungry we ate three hotdogs and I don't know how many french fries."

"We were soaking wet and that creep in the restaurant – what was his name?"

Momo was dreaming all alone, leaving Gigi to struggle with a memory that seemed to have changed with time into a nightmare: "He was lookin' at us shaking like leaves and laughing."

"It didn't stop us from feeling good. Do you still like french fries as much as you used to?"

With her gown wrapped around her as tightly as the skin of a bear Gigi seemed to be counting each tap made by her

46

heels as she walked from one wall to the other, thinking, "It could'a worked out if crazy Momo hadn't got the bright idea of turning himself into a robber so he could give me presents, but it's true I'm the one that was pushing him to earn money instead of spending his time throwing knives into barn doors or doing little jobs that hardly paid nothing, just enough to go to the Café Central for a meal every once in a while." She remembered the evening he'd come to the restaurant, proud of what he'd done, and invited her not to the cornfield this time but to the stuffy little shack his father had left him when he decided to freeze to death beside his double-barrelled hunting rifle, likely the same one Momo had used to get the money from a storekeeper in Laurierville, he hadn't said which one right away, "But what got into me to go and tell papa about it? It's as if I was trying to get rid of him and counting on papa to turn him over to the cops."

She started as she heard Momo saying, in a tone that bordered on indifference, almost mocking: "You told yourself that Momo could cool his heels in that hole all by himself. It didn't have nothing to do with you, whatever happened to me, cause I hadn't done it for you, I suppose?" His elbow was stuck in the pillow and he was stretched out on his side, a cigarette in the corner of his mouth, contrary to his usual habit of sticking it right in the middle of his mouth. She stopped walking to look at him, not understanding how she could feel nothing for him, neither love nor disgust – nothing. A kind of vague boredom. Only eagerness to see him disappear from her life. He went on in the same neutral tone, detached, rather mocking, as though he were a stranger to it all, as though he were simply remarking on a fact, and that was the first thing she had liked about him before it started getting on her nerves, the nonchalance that followed his moments of rage; she thought, "He gets that from his big brother. I feel sorry for the woman that would'a had to wipe their behinds all her life." Then she rushed over to the little bedside table, suddenly panic-stricken:

47

Nine o'clock and the other one was on his way!

"Listen Momo, that's all very nice, the good old days, the time we did it in the field, but these days I don't live off of love and cold water."

"You don't have to tell me that. You want me to clear out, right?"

She didn't stir, just waited for him to comply; but he was in no hurry to leave, and he went on: "I don't have no rights, eh, an old buddy from back home? Come on, Reddy, I still got a little money."

"That's what you think."

"My money ain't no good?"

She stared at him, not considering the risk she was taking by confronting him: "You can't even get it up! Because I sleep with anybody, is that why? Don't be scared to admit it. Anyway, the only thing I'm asking you is to get rid of that big lump you left in my bathtub. Now move it!" He got up, his legs outside the bed, brutally aroused from his indifference. "Okay, Reddy, I'll do it. Don't start yelling. I'll screw up your plans if I stick around, right? You figured I was gonna play dead when I got out. Well, you can forget about that. Don't say nothing. I wasn't gone very long before you went running after the first stud that come along in a Triumph."

"If you think you're telling me something I don't know... I knew you'd show up one of these days, even if you had to cross the desert. Not because I mean nothing special to you. Just to bug me. Get even with me."

He raised his head, innocent as a lamb: "Get even for what?" She stood on tiptoe, arms folded across her chest, out of breath before she even started to talk: "I wanted to live, can you understand? I would'a been an old maid before you made up your mind to do something. Sneak off and freeze our asses in some shack that stinks of I don't know what. Not even knowing what was gonna happen to us. Watch you sharpening your goddamn knives, that's one hell of a life!" She was silent, watching the alarm clock as

48

Momo slipped a dollar bill under it, "for your trouble."

"Son of a bitch!"

She was about to throw herself on him when someone knocked on the door, twice, close together. Momo sat up on the edge of the bed, blinking because of the smoke. "Well, go and answer it!" he ordered her; she was still standing in front of him, red as a beet.

6

Momo finally stopped, out of breath, in the grey dawn that was as misty and silent as the autumn woods, just long enough for his breathing to slow down and his lungs to stop burning; he looked at the sky, low between the walls of the houses, still untouched by the first rays of light, and although he looked all around him he saw nothing, not even a taxi. He supposed that he was walking on the big street – as he had baptised rue Sainte-Catherine – because the restaurants had given way to stores, all closed now. He breathed calmly, his parka wide open, arms at his sides, waiting for the old man coming up to him who seemed to be swimming in his too large overcoat. Momo blocked his way on the sidewalk. The old man raised his head, a dirty hand rummaging through the nicotine-stained beard, dragging his stiff leg. "Where's the Paradise?" Momo asked, realizing that his question was out of place, but he repeated it so insistently that it seemed dangerous not to reply, in spite of Momo's small size, or so the old man must have thought as he kept licking his cracked lips with a thick white tongue, pointing over his shoulder towards the west. Momo aped him furiously, holding out his own hand, shaking it for a moment before he clutched the old man's shoulder; the latter, without turning his head or covering his mouth with his hand, began to cough so violently that Momo pushed him away. The old man almost lost his footing and as soon as he could move his stiff leg he spat on the sidewalk, then shouted in Momo's direction: "It's closed now anyway. Everything's closed now!" Momo walked along the sidewalk where there wasn't even an inch of snow left. He didn't feel like having cold feet inside his already wet boots.

In too much of a hurry to button his parka, he felt the cold grip his sweating body the way it did whenever he'd tied one on the night before, and if he wasn't really running it was because he was trying to figure out, not why he was going to the Paradise, but just what had happened between the time somebody had knocked at the door twice and the time he had abruptly awakened, stretched out on Gigi's bed with all his clothes on, seeing the naked leg on the horizon marked off by the edge of the mattress. As he raised himself on his elbow, heavy-headed, he had stared rather long at the rest of the body which he saw from behind, thinking, heart pounding: "It can't be, it can't, I must be having a bad dream," but there was no possible doubt after he got up, still dazed, and he had to admit that it was indeed true and, into the bargain, it was his own switch-blade sticking out between her shoulder-blades; the dressing-gown crumpled around her, darkened with blood. His vision was blurred; he picked up his parka and, running, threw the bottle of rye, which rolled over to the door. He went down the stairs without a thought for the noise he was making, thinking of just one thing: the snow where he could vomit, empty himself at last. He felt his stomach heave but there was no relief as he trembled, frozen to the marrow, telling himself that she was cold now too, and that her mouth, open but forever silent, was not breathing now, but as empty as the neck of a bottle. And that her eye was staring at the bed where he had slept, snoring in all innocence, more powerless than the alarm clock, "at least," he thought, "if it'd been my fault . . . If I could just remember what we did after that little game of poker. Reddy went looking for that goddamn bottle of perfume and she squirted it all over the place, in my hair, my armpits, and then *m'sieu le curé* got up with a long face, like he wasn't used to having a drink that way, in the middle of the night, and went away with his tail between his legs. Reddy wanted me to untie big Gène but I don't know what got into me, I was just like jelly, and then I fell over like a rock. I must'a been passed out all that time, but how the hell did it happen? I don't know . . ." He came to the corner of Sainte-Catherine and Saint-Laurent, and moving instinctively, very fast, he felt around in his pocket for the bone handle, which reassured him, as he understood suddenly why he had decided to run to the Paradise after leaving Gigi's place – he'd been positive the guilty party must be Nico or one of his men; the proof was the switch-blade they'd stolen from him the night they beat him up and dumped him in a garbage can, but "that don't prove nothing," he thought, "nobody's gonna believe it," and he was frightened. As he approached the Paradise he could feel it inside him, enormous, a fear not so much of confronting them but of being taken for the murderer, "That'd look good, a guy that kills his girlfriend out of jealousy, you see that every day, and I must'a left some traces," but he had no intention of going back to check on the spot, and see Gigi's wide-spread legs again, her bare buttocks and the knife pinning her to the floor, her motionless eyes staring at the foot of the bed. His shoulder was starting to ache again. The nightclub was closed; no light came through the rectangular window. "Looks like I'm gonna have to spend the whole day waiting for those bastards!" He had spoken aloud, not so much to be heard, if that were possible, but to suppress the viscous invasion of fear. He looked at the still cloudy sky, sniffed and kicked at a garbage can turned over on a snowbank. "If you guys think you're gonna get me like that!" he shouted one last time before starting down Saint-Laurent, urged on, as he felt, by his desire to disappear, go back to Saint-Emmanuel, "sure it's a hole, but at least there's peace and quiet," but he was also thinking that never again would he be at peace, no matter where he went, at least not until he knew exactly what had happened, not until he'd found someone who would pay for everything, for Gigi's death and for the fear that was gripping at his belly and throat. All he'd needed was to run into Nico, Vic or Frenchy, anybody, when he left Gigi's place. He walked down the street, not knowing where he was going, "mustn't go to my room," he thought, "you never know, maybe *m'sieu* talked, or big Gène."

He needed a smoke, his teeth were chattering and he kept walking mechanically, as though his legs were disjointed. He opened the door of a little snack bar where a solitary man was reading his paper, sitting on a stool in front of his cup of coffee, responding with a nod to the chatter of the waitress, a woman of uncertain age, her frizzy blonde hair black at the roots. He walked along the counter, hesitated at a table, then sat at the very back, behind the chrome rack where the waitress's imitation fur coat was hanging, waiting for her to come and ask him what he wanted; he wasn't hungry though, or rather he felt incapable of swallowing anything at all, too absorbed in his ruminations, too busy remembering what had happened after the skinny character left, blushing in his white shirt buttoned all the way up to the neck, tieless; he had blushed and stammered excuses when he came in, too, at the sight of Momo sprawled on the bed, hiding his swollen black eye behind his hand. And Gigi apologizing for the untidiness, not daring to make introductions while the client stuck his long nervous hands into his overcoat pockets and Momo examined the square chin, the heavy black eyebrows that formed a long bar above his eyes, the short hair that had grown in without completely concealing the tonsure, a scar Momo had spotted as soon as the other man turned around to close the door; it made him smile, and the defrocked priest turned red with shame when he noticed it.

"Toast and coffee and a large Export."

"Nothing else?"

"If I want something else I'll let you know, okay?" Momo

53

replied, annoyed, anxious for her to disappear behind her counter.

She turned away, sullen, and Momo had to hold himself back to keep from giving her a good swat on her protruding rump, squeezed into a black skirt that was worn shiny and so short you could see her flowered underpants when she bent over to pick up a coin; she slipped it into the pocket of her white blouse that was just sheer enough to give the illusion that the coin was a nipple. The coffee was scalding and he breathed in its steam, thinking of his father who every morning drank his boiling tea from a white granite mug with a blue rim, standing silently in front of the stove, his mind elsewhere, likely with the woman who appeared in the single wedding picture, rather dreamy, with long hair as black as her eyes; she had gone away one May night when Momo was only a baby, a scandal so outrageous that the abandoned husband couldn't get work to feed his two orphans as they were called; that made it easier for him to keep house, they said, something the faithless woman would never have done; since her disappearance she had been referred to as the wild Indian, because as far back as anyone could remember such a thing had never happened or even been heard of. So his father hardly went out, except to go to the general store where they gave him scraps of meat, or to sit in his chair on the gallery overlooking the cemetery just behind the church, no longer expecting anything, so it seemed, looking as passive as an old woman resigned to solitude, a little ridiculous too with the apron cut out of an old pair of overalls that he wore around his waist from morning to night, his face glowing from the heat of the stove; and because over the years his manners had become very cautious, almost fearful, the young people called him Old Lady Boulanger. He couldn't fix the leaky roof, replace the stovepipe or even hammer a nail in properly: Calixa or Momo always had to do it. And the day Calixa headed off for the woods for good, his sack on his back, he'd started to whimper, and without turning around

54

Calixa had told him: "Act like a man if you don't want Momo to be ashamed of his father." Momo had burst out laughing, he remembered as though it were yesterday, and said: "It's too late for that," and the last words had been too much; the next day when Momo got up to go to the saw-mill he didn't see his father standing in front of the stove or sitting in the rocking-chair between the stove and the door. Two days and still no news. Then Calixa brought him back, stiff as a fence post, completely frozen, a little less like an old woman without his apron and with his features contorted. All Calixa knew was that he must have been over-come by the cold as he slept next to his rifle; no one mentioned the yellowing wedding picture found in his shirt pocket and which Momo threw into the fire, he still wondered why as he sipped at the hot coffee which had stopped the chattering of his teeth, thinking: "I didn't cry that time, oh no, I never cried once in my whole goddamn bitch of a life," and even when he recalled the dressing-gown crumpled around the knife, Gigi's open mouth, no tears came to his eyes, just a wrenching sensation in his belly at the thought of having to go back behind bars for the rest of his life, "if the big guy decides to talk." And he didn't under-stand Gène's disappearance; he'd been tied to the tap, "unless," he thought, "Reddy untied him while I was asleep, that could be." The waitress smiled at him, her broad powdered face resting on her too plump hands, "they're fatter than mine," placing his own on the table near the coffee cup, empty except for a little thick sugary syrup, wondering if those hands could have...No, because the knife between Gigi's shoulder-blades hadn't been in his possession after Nico stuck it in his own pocket – he couldn't consider himself guilty, although as he thought about it he felt responsible in some way for what had hap-pened, just because he'd been there, sleeping in an alcoholic stupor. He said, a little too loud, it seemed: "Fine fucking state of affairs, they take advantage of her and then do that to her, the sons of bitches!" The waitress was still smiling at him and as he was looking at her foolishly, she stuck out her tongue, "it's long enough for me to lie down on," he thought as he returned the gesture. The radio was blaring. He lit a cigarette, after glancing at the untouched slices of toast, the globs of butter now solid and cold. He put on his parka, holding out his hand as though to avoid falling. "You look like you could use a pick-me-up," the waitress said, "you look a little weak in the knees." He simply stared at her with his good eye and she looked down at the cash register.

7

His toes were squeezed inside the soaking-wet boots which
flopped through the dirty melting snow, but he was beginning to feel warm as he walked the crowded streets, in spite
of the damp cold and the impression he had of wandering
down a corridor that opened onto other corridors. Blasts of
steam came out of doors as they were opened; people went
inside, others came out, looking absent-minded, and others
like him simply dawdled, warming the air with their
breath. He thought: "The city isn't so bad, you know, you
can get by." He pressed his nose against a window that had
a display of huge photographs, almost lifesize, representing
men's bodies tattooed with all sorts of designs, arabesques
encrusted on their flesh, like the dragon on the broad chest
of a bald man with a ring in one ear, and he was wondering
if it hurt to be marked like that and how long the scars of
the operation would stay on the flesh when he shivered as
he felt someone's breath on him. He turned around – an
about-face so sudden that his forehead bumped into the
chin of a young man, twenty-five years old perhaps, freshly
shaven, his white skin made slightly pink by his shaving
lotion, blond hair drifting around his ears, who smiled at
him and asked, "Want to buy me a drink?" Only that, with
an impudent smile. Momo raised his hand as though to
force him to step back, unable to think of anything better to
do, not even one of those fast answers that would have shut

57

him up. The blond stepped back, still smiling: "Looks like you got up on the wrong side of the bed this morning." Momo took one step, saying to himself: "Fuck off, cocksucker!" but the blond walked away, as affected as Marlene in spite of his jeans, his open black leather jacket and his boots with their chains scraping the pavement under the soft snow. Momo stood there, not really angry, just thinking about anything to make him forget what was waiting for him, though he knew he'd been looking for it ever since he'd been let out, since he'd gone to see Gigi's father instead of going home after Ti-Pit had told him the only news that mattered to him: that Gigi had gone to the city. He had gone up the hill, avoiding the village, happy to be walking as he'd always done, and checking that the money he'd pinned under the lining of his parka before his arrest was still there. The woods smelled of rotting vegetation. Usually at this time of year he would have been hunting rabbits and partridge, "but I had other business to take care of"; when he reached the top of the mountain he saw smoke between the trees, and knew that Phonse was home; he felt apprehensive about the violence, turned bitter by months of waiting, for which he had to find some relief so he could regain his old nonchalance, a sort of indifference like his brother Calixa's. Phonse had let him in, not seeming particularly suspicious, but still surprised to see him apparently unchanged, as rude and foolish as ever. He slammed the door behind him. "Surprise, eh, you old bugger?" He looked around the room: it was fairly large but low, the walls covered with old painted cardboard, marked with rings that made him say: "Looks like you piss on the walls instead of in the sink like everybody else!" Phonse was stooping, not proud of his height as he used to be; it even seemed to embarrass him, as he slumped into the old springless armchair to make himself as small as possible; the chair was just behind the kitchen table so that he could see the highway, a poor distraction because even the milkman stopped coming up after All Saint's Day. He likely

58

hadn't seen Momo coming, otherwise he wouldn't have let him in, "and I'd'a had to kick the door down," Momo thought, smiling as he noted the disastrous effect his visit was having on his "father-in-law." They listened to the creaking of the old clock, Phonse scrunched down in his chair, eyes lowered, and Momo standing, rolling a cigarette. "So," Phonse began, "you done your time. Goes fast, eh?" With no apparent irony, a sigh in his voice. He seemed to realize that time was passing. And Momo replied, "Yeah, here I am, and I need some help. I came to see my father-in-law as fast as I could." He paused to light his cigarette and step on the match. "Maybe I shouldn't'a, eh? I heard you weren't too anxious to find out what was happening to me, but it was just trouble-makers that said that. If you listen to what everybody's got to say you just end up making yourself sick..." Phonse kept his eyes obstinately lowered as though he weren't there, his hands spread across the arms of the chair; Momo went on in the same dull, rather tense voice: "I wanna see Reddy; I hear she's gone off to the city since the last time we seen each other. She's been dying to for years. I ain't blaming you, I know you couldn't'a stopped her even if you told her not to go. You must be glad she's got herself a good set-up in the city. But I want her address and don't try and tell me you ain't heard from her." The only reply was the three dry notes of the cuckoo clock. "Listen, old man, it looks like you forgot one thing: it's your fault I had to kill all that goddamn time behind bars. You made me waste enough time already, so snap it up!" Phonse barely moved his hands, which he had slipped between his thighs to warm them, saying very quietly: "I ain't gettin mixed up in that business." "Don't treat me like some kind'a idiot. Reddy was the only person that knew about it; I don't know why she told you. I shouldn't'a said nothing. But that's all water under the bridge and I don't wanna talk about it no more. All I want's her address. Now move it."

He put his hand around the flame of a match he'd lit for

no apparent reason, just for the hell of it; leaning slightly against the wall, shoulders hunched, he moved his hand until the flame made the thin, greyish curtain tremble where it fell a couple of inches from the peeling paint of the window sill. Phonse finally looked up, miserable, his lower lip not touching the upper one and trembling as though his words, until then, had been only inaudible vibrations. Momo brought the flame closer to the curtain, which was slowly turning yellow. "I don't get it," he said, his face creased by the effort. Phonse got out of his chair, his clenched fists on the big arborite table with rings burned on it by the bottoms of saucepans, and looked at Momo with something the latter interpreted as fiercer than hate; his eyelids slightly lowered over the grey liquid of his eyes, he stared at Momo the way Gigi did later when he slipped the money under her alarm clock. The steady gaze chilled him: he felt more than simple hatred – he felt eliminated in some way, stricken from the world of the living, excluded from the human race without a word. But it seemed to him just then that although he was defenceless against the decree, everything was becoming easier, because he was talking to the real Phonse, the one who had turned him in not out of concern for justice or for reasons of conscience, but simply so he wouldn't have to see him prowling around, even if Gigi followed the first person who showed up and disappeared from the village forever. Momo had something to say to Phonse, to ask rather, certain of obtaining satisfaction for the simple reason that Phonse owed him something for sending him off to cool his heels behind bars; he'd been away just long enough to be able to bear Phonse's look now, even force him to lower his eyes; it was a revenge he'd dreamed about when he was inside, as he dreamed about humiliating Gigi afterwards. But though Phonse had responded to Momo's hatred and lowered his eyes, he got to his feet now with what was left of his self-respect: "Leave my girl alone. Ain't you screwed up her life enough as it is?" Momo dropped the burned-up match: "Her address."

60

Phonse uttered a long plaintive sigh, tired of resisting – defeated once when his moist eyes were unable to hold onto his daughter, swooning over the man he referred to as the "fashion-plate," and now again not so much by Momo's insistence as by the fact that he owed him something. He opened the glass door of the china cabinet, took the cover off a roasting pan he used as a catch-all and finally recognized, by touch, his one and only letter from his daughter. "I don't know how glad Gigi's gonna be to hear from you," he said in a voice that was almost compassionate. "Anyway, here's her address. Here," and he held out the torn envelope, after taking out the letter, a single sheet of lined paper from a school-child's scribbler. Momo checked that the address was legible, noticing out of the corner of his eye the trembling of Phonse's big spotted hand, which hung suspended in the air. He waited for it to fall, motionless, alongside Phonse's leg, before saying: "Great. I can give her a message from you at the same time. You got any news for her?" Phonse shook his head, his hand on his flat skull where a single tuft of white hair still grew obstinately, then Momo went out, closing the door harder than he'd intended. As he went down the hill that wound between the trees to the heart of the village he didn't once turn around, though he was positive that eyes were following him, at least as far as the sudden turn that marked the town limits; but he was relieved of the bitterness cultivated for so long in the void where he had stagnated those last months, relieved to the point of smiling at the tin roofs gleaming white in the bright winter sun. He had already forgotten his visit to Phonse, imagining himself walking along big city streets looking for Gigi, passing the Hôtel without going in as he had at first intended, opening the door of the Café Central. Marie-Rose nearly jumped over the counter when she saw him: "Hey! If it ain't Momo!" He had been expecting a cold reception and couldn't get over seeing her dance for joy as she repeated, "It's been ages. You want a coffee? Some honey doughnuts? They're fresh."

61

He stopped in front of a window to look at a mannequin that reminded him of Marie-Rose and the hints sprinkled through her chatter, while he ate a sticky *ragoût de boulettes,* "still, it's better than the garbage they used to give us inside," he thought. Then she had brought him a piece of *tarte au sucre,* constantly telling him, "we missed you so much, Momo," even adding, "A bird in the hand's worth two in the bush," insinuating that as far as she was concerned she was quite prepared to be that one. He also remembered her way of fiddling with the button of her dark brown sweater, which fit so tightly that her breasts stuck out in points when she stood up. He began to feel sorry he'd left as soon as he finished his meal, and got on the bus only to realize, once he was with Gigi, that he no longer really felt like making her pay for what she'd done to him; he wouldn't even have shown his annoyance if he'd been able to get it up like a normal man. That was what had infuriated him, and the fact that he'd started to think about the men who had paraded into her bed while he was serving his sentence, through her fault, not his; and he thought, "She must'a thought I was no good and she died with that idea still in her head." He gritted his teeth, still shivering despite the coffee he'd just drunk, then turned around and went into a delicatessen where he sat down without taking off his parka for fear of losing the slight warmth. The Greek who brought him his smoked meat with French fries had skin that looked almost black against his white uniform: "Snowing again," he sighed, slipping the bill under the plate. "And there wasn't even an inch on the ground when I got out," Momo thought, just to think of anything at all; but immediately he remembered the skinny client, awkward, not knowing where to put his long hands, staring at the ceiling; he'd felt, like Gigi, that there was one person too many in the room that was made for two. With the remains of his tonsure, come here to find some diversion, as he admitted later when Gigi apologized for receiving him with one of her cousins there, constantly blushing and scratching his scalp, until Momo suggested a game of poker. All three were silent, even when *m'sieu le curé* opened the bottle of rye that was weighing down the pocket of his overcoat, and they played in all seriousness, Momo sitting with his back against the head of the bed, Gigi Indian fashion in the middle of the bed, and *m'sieu le curé* very erect, his legs together. Momo doubled his bet and won two times out of three. There was a sound – the rustling of the shower curtain – and Momo shut the bathroom door, ignoring *m'sieu le curé*'s worried look. Gigi dropped a glass and it broke between her feet. Momo said, "We'll drink it straight." They started the game again as they drank, and a little later, slightly drunk, they drank right from the bottle, passing it to one another with almost mechanical regularity. Momo was dripping sweat. Gigi got up and rummaged in a drawer under a pile of underwear for a can of deodorant spray which she aimed at him, making him raise his arms – and he laughed, the cold spray tickled, even felt good. And then she had to say it, with a total stranger as witness, as though she couldn't help herself: "He stinks if we don't spray him every once in a while." That was too much; he snatched the spray can from her hands, stared at *m'sieu le curé:* "If a girl goes out with a guy for years – even sleeps with him – and then when he's away she decides to go with somebody else, a total stranger, in a brand-new sports car, what do you think of that?" Now he didn't have to look at the ceiling or scratch his tonsure; he had his five cards to stare at, holding them out of the range of their vision, examining them as though to escape the need to intervene but still stammering a confused response – Momo grasped only that he was in no situation to pass judgement, since he came here to take advantage of Mademoiselle Gigi's misfortune, while he could have amused himself otherwise, he said, blushing, speaking to Gigi who was affecting a sort of fondness for the bottle wedged between her thigh and her calf. There was a long, numb silence – then suddenly, seized with remorse, *m'sieu le curé* added that a girl who does that must have good reasons, otherwise she must certainly be a person who – how could he put it – was rather frivolous. Momo sniffed with annoyance and his laughter rang false: "You call that frivolous?" And he pointed at Gigi. "Any idiot can see you ain't the guy that's been stabbed in the back. And you don't know the whole story. But I'm gonna tell you one thing, *m'sieu le curé,* and that's that any girl you can get with the sound of a motor, she's what I'd call cheap. Whadda you think, Reddy? You aren't saying nothing."

She threw her cards in his face and jumped off the bed. *M'sieu le curé* looked down, seemed to reflect before he spoke, smiling a little awkwardly: "You remind me of a pair of lovers quarrelling over nothing." Gigi picked up the bottle from the bed as though she hadn't heard and took a good long drink before putting it down on the dresser, a lock of hair clinging to her forehead; then, with no thought for her open dressing-gown, she came over to the bed, arms crossed on her chest, on the point of tossing off some cool retort that stayed stuck in her throat or lower down in her chest, compressed between her arms where her fingernails were digging in, making white lines. Finally, glaring, she said they were both disgusting, putting them and all their kind in the same bag. Then, turning on her heels, she went and leaned against the dresser, hands clutching the bottle from which she seemed to be drawing the air she lacked.

The smoked meat was too fat for Momo; he took the sandwich apart to remove the lean meat and swallowed it without chewing. Eating relieved his stomach ache. He soaked the rye bread in his coffee. She didn't drink back in the days when she was Phonse's girl, any more than she wore lipstick or powder. He would have liked to tell her to let go of the bottle, he even got up intending to ask her to forget all this and to live as she pleased. Elbows leaning on the dresser, she looked thirstily at the bottle which was only a third full of lukewarm rye. And Momo had the impression she was laughing softly without really laughing, a laugh that shook her shoulders and made her long red hair wave, when *m'sieu le curé,* staggering on his long legs, raised his voice as though someone were asking him something: "Say there, lovebirds, don't forget about me now." He said no more, nor did he make another move, too surprised when he got a punch in the nose for any reaction but painful and silent astonishment. "Get outta here! We seen enough of you for one day," Momo shouted, throwing the priest's overcoat and hat which he had been bending over to pick up. He opened the door with the hand that held the overcoat, his hat pulled down over his forehead, and looked at them for a moment before he disappeared. Momo kicked the door shut, went over and stood behind Gigi, not daring to stop or put his hand on her shoulder, or to say something in a voice that would be different from the one he knew – something like "forget it, Reddy, I'm gonna," but it didn't work, coming from him it seemed crazy. And yet that was what he was trying to wring out of his confusion, words to deliver both of them, but instead he stepped on his cigarette, more and more furious at just standing there behind her, saying nothing, and looking at her trembling shoulders. "Listen here, Reddy," he said in a dry voice that sounded imperious and irritating even to him, "I'm gonna go now, I just got one thing to look after here in town and then you'll never see my face again, never. I didn't come here to bug you." And she, who had been waiting only for that, began to shout: "Why did you do it then? Why?" He saw her face, grimacing and aged, the tendon in her neck standing out under the skin and, most of all, the bright bloodshot eyes, and he heard himself say in a voice that was almost supplicating: "I don't know, I really don't...To see if it was really over." She regurgitated the rye she had just swallowed, laughing like a madwoman: "If you wanna know if it's over, well it is! You didn't have to come here to find that out. You're so jealous, what do you think...You'd'a liked to knock off all my clients and then expect me to get down on my knees and say I'm sorry. Don't try and tell me nothing different." He didn't answer;

his head was spinning, the room was whirling, and the bottle he'd picked up had slipped from his hands. "Clumsy bastard!" Gigi shouted, but it didn't matter to him if she shouted, called him whatever she wanted, if only the room would stop spinning. He stepped back and the edge of the bed struck his legs. She told him to leave, but he slumped down, his cheek against the cool cards.

8

He looked over the storekeeper's fat, hairy hand and tried to make out the numbers he was writing on a bit of crumpled wrapping paper, the glasses with their heavy black frames slipping to the end of his nose, and then Momo's eyes began imperceptibly to wander towards the two hunting knives and the machete, a fairly faithful copy of the one used by explorers in the bush; he weighed it in his hand for a long time before replacing it in its stiff leather sheath, thinking that such a sharp, heavy blade would be as good as an axe. "Thirteen sixteen, please," the big man finally said, in English, as he wrapped up the knives and the machete, while Momo stood motionless as though he hadn't expected to spend any money at all. *"Treize piasses et seize,"* he repeated it in French this time, staring at Momo over his glasses. Momo twisted his body, his left hand rummaging inside the lining of his parka. He sighed as he touched the wad of bills pinned inside, peeled one off without looking to see what denomination it was. It was a ten. He removed another and placed it on the counter, watching the large hairy hand smooth out the imperturbable face of Elizabeth the Second. He picked up his package and as he was about to turn around he thought of the change the salesman had given and motioned to a camouflage hood on a hanger; he imagined himself going into the Paradise in a few hours, or to the Café Central or the Hôtel du Nord if he

67

decided to take the bus to Saint-Emmanuel where the empty shack was waiting for him – and the white granite mug, the cemetery behind the church, all that; it seemed so far away now, Marie-Rose herself with the smile that said many things – he saw himself arriving unexpectedly, early in the evening, wearing this grey-green disguise with its mouldy yellow spots; he would stick the machete into the floor between his feet to show that he was back and had a good one to tell them: poor old Reddy who wanted so much to live in the city, and now she was dead, he thought of telling them: especially Phonse who had let her go without knowing or even suspecting what was in store for her, she who could be had so easily. And she'd been had very often, and he'd say so, even if Phonse yelled like a lunatic. But something was bothering him, keeping him here on the muddy streets, not just his desire to pay them back for the beating they'd given him, the pains in his shoulder, the right arm which still hurt, the black eye: it was, rather, the fear of being taken for someone who was easily scared, to say nothing of the fact that going away like that, with one of his knives in his girlfriend's back, would look suspicious if the police had followed him. Besides, he had the unpleasant impression of being the victim of a put-up job the extent of which escaped him. When you've done time in jail it's hard to play the innocent. The parcel he was carrying began to feel heavy. He touched the bone handle in his pocket, thinking: "That's a pretty good start, a tool like that," and he looked around for some place to hide his parcel. Saint-Laurent wasn't an ordinary street – nothing but restaurants, greasy spoons that stank of hot fat, a movie-house with gaudy posters, not the slightest hiding-place. "Anyway, I can't just drop my bundle like that!" And then as he was looking in the window of a restaurant he noticed Frenchy, his nose stuck in a club sandwich, the round head with its bristly hair, the coarse face that still wasn't shaved at four o'clock in the afternoon. He stood there frozen, listening to himself rage inside: at first he felt his heart pound, then he was overcome by fear, and he looked at the passers-by taking long steps into the cold wind. He was panting. As he stood in front of the window looking at Frenchy, he thought: "Good thing I seen you, buddy, I just about took off and we never would'a had the chance to have our little talk."

As he moved back he bumped into the pedestal of a huge pay-scale on which someone had stuck the picture of a girl naked to the navel and he waited until he was alone so he could hide his parcel behind it, then went back and leaned against the wall which formed a kind of lobby in front of the entrance, where he could keep an eye on Frenchy, "as innocent as a baby with his fingers in the till!" he said, loud enough to make a passer-by turn his head, not catching his indignant look, too distracted by his own voluptuous jubilation, "that's right, buddy, eat while you still got the chance," and he gripped the bone handle, the bumps on its surface sticking into his damp skin, a sensation he had felt before, along with the same feverish pleasure, the same excitement, which reminded him of a late afternoon in October, just at twilight, when he'd gone into a hardware store in Laurierville five minutes before closing, up to the counter where a short man with greying hair was putting away gallon cans of paint. His legs were rubbery, his arm stiff in his pocket and he could barely see through his dark glasses; he tried to speak firmly with no chance of being contradicted: "Give me everything you got in the till there, pop, and make it fast." The man turned around calmly, as though he were dealing with an ordinary customer, and for a second Momo thought there was someone else behind him; he didn't turn around, although he felt a strong urge to do so. The man rubbed his hands on his canvas apron, looking at him without quite realizing he was there to collect the day's receipts. And to remind him, as well as to pull himself out of the uncertainty which was gripping both of them, Momo pulled his father's cap down over his forehead; it pinched his head so tight he could feel the blood throbbing in his temples, and he took his left hand out of his pocket. The click of the knife made the man start and he kept repeating as though Momo were any ordinary customer: "What can I do for you?"

"The money, and make it fast."

Not another word, for fear of giving himself away, of showing by the trembling in his voice that he was nothing but a country boy, an easily outwitted amateur. The man was squat, shorter than Momo, and so calm Momo had to threaten him with his knife. "Snap it up!" Momo shouted, a lump in his throat, and the man nodded, then pushed a button on the cash register that sounded to Momo like an explosion. He walked behind the counter and took the bills out from under the springs that held them in place, still pointing his knife at the man, who had now slipped his hands into his apron pockets and was saying, in his calm, almost conciliatory manner: "If I was you, my boy, I wouldn't touch nothing."

"And if I was you," Momo replied, "I wouldn't say another goddamn word."

Momo stuffed the bills into his pockets, then picked up the telephone and cut the wire with his knife; he ran towards the door, which closed slowly behind him. He didn't stop until he was on his way out of town, in the cold and the dark, having got rid of his dark glasses and his cap, not sure he was safe behind the post that marked the bus stop. His heart was pounding. And he asked himself how he had got it into his head to take the bus as though nothing had happened, just when everybody was going back to the village, remembering at once that it was precisely because no one with any sense would have imagined him taking flight like this, going home by bus. He didn't have long to worry; seven or eight minutes later big Jérôme's rickety old bus stopped with a shriek of twisted metal. Emilien was driving, one hand on the wheel, the other between his thighs in an unsuccessful attempt to hide the bottle of beer which, theoretically, shouldn't have been there. "Yeah,"

Momo thought, "but take away the beer and you ain't got a driver." He sat just behind Emilien on one of the stiff straw seats that burned the behinds of passengers from the city. "Still chasin' after the girls, eh Momo? Aren't you scared Gigi's gonna make a scene? She might start lookin' around, too." Momo laughed with Emilien, longer than usual, as though this laughter signified a return to normality, the sudden breaking of the knot that was choking him and his final victory over his fear. The bus jolted along the ruts left from last winter, but he let himself be tossed about, his hand clutching the wad of crumpled bills in his pocket, imagining her surprise when he piled them on the table, how impossible she would find it to reproach him for the way he'd earned the money, since she'd told him more and more often, with a kind of nagging vehemence: "If you're any kind'a man get me outta this hole, I don't care how. I'm fed up with this kind'a life, stuck away here; I wanta go to the city." He had told himself that with money, quite a lot of money, he could indulge some of her whims, and then maybe she'd forget her idea of going away, which made no sense to him, quite content as he was with the smell of sawdust, waiting long hours in the woods and the pleasure of hunting. That very evening, before he sat down across from her at the Café Central, he took from his pocket a large roll of bills held together by a rubber band, saying in the most natural way imaginable: "Here, go buy yourself a dress or whatever you want." She was speechless, as though it were somehow unbelievable to see him associated with so much money. "Next time," he added, "I'll buy you a ticket to Miami, if that's what you want." But she still hadn't recovered, saying: "How come, Momo?" not touching the roll of money, even with her fingertips, as it sat there between them like something that had nothing to do with either of them. "Go on, take it," Momo said, "or I'm scared it'll disappear as fast as I got it." And he sat there, a twelve-cent cigar between his teeth. "Where'd you get all that money?" She was as white as a sheet, unable to stop con-

71

templating the twenty-dollar bill that covered the other denominations. He arranged his thin lips in a smile, his teeth showing slightly. "You done something bad, eh?" He was still smiling, not out of indifference or bravado, but to put on a good show; then he lit his cigar and she choked on the smoke. He felt above her concerns, and even though she refused to touch the money he thought that for once she was seeing him in another light, the proper one this time. It was later, one evening, when he was coming out of her, that he told her everything, omitting the cold sweat of fear that had streamed from his armpits. "You're crazy, Momo, taking a chance like that, you could go to jail," but she spoke without conviction, almost proud of him. He shouldn't have sniffed with satisfaction then; she had punished him by examining the sheets: "I'd like to know how you get your sheets so dirty. Look at that yellow spot!" And she stuck the large stain on the pillow-case in his face with the same profoundly offended air as the night before when she sprayed him with that pine-scented perfume, saying he stank: "Your Indian blood, eh?" This allusion to his mother, to the unknown woman who had disappeared from his life before he really knew about things, was the only offence that wounded him to the point of silence and indifference. For three days he didn't even give her a sign of life, too humiliated to feel the slightest desire to see her or touch her. And after he came back from the woods, only because of physical desire, things hadn't been the same. She had changed too, and was irritated equally by his silence and his way of talking.

He had to step aside to let two customers go past, and that made him lose sight of Frenchy, still sitting at the table, off in the clouds apparently, but Momo, sure he couldn't be seen, didn't budge, scarcely looking up when he noticed the waitress leaning over Frenchy who seemed to be pinching her shoulder. Momo laughed unpleasantly, thinking: "That's right, do it while you still can," then he saw Frenchy get up, pick up his black leather coat and follow

72

the waitress. "Go and sing your little song," Momo told himself, stepping back so he was invisible, wondering if it wouldn't be better to go inside and catch him in the act at the urinal, but his instincts told him to stay where he was, leaning against the cement wall, his nervous trembling gone as though the knowledge it would soon be over had removed him in advance from what might, was even bound to happen. He felt as though he were on the look-out for something, as sure of getting Frenchy as he was of shooting a partridge he'd caught napping in a clearing. The cold was dense, liquid almost, permeating his clothes, his flesh and his bones. His hands felt fleshless, reduced to bones and nerves. He nibbled at the scab on his throbbing lip. He used his right hand to take a cigarette out of a package and light it, glad to be able to check its flexibility in spite of the pain that shot along the nerve in his wrist, thinking: "Good thing my left hand's still okay," and he gripped the bone handle, a reassuring extension of his hand; he remembered how he would crucify a hare or stab a partridge while other men, disguised as hunters, spent hours beating the bushes and terrifying the game which escaped from their shots, finally returning to the Hôtel with long faces, claiming there wasn't a single goddamn animal left in the country, "and they call themselves hunters, those good-for-nothin' drunks," except for Calixa who lived off his rifle all year long, off his rifle and the sale of the *caribou* Gros-Jos picked up in some clandestine distillery. He was amazed to be so distant from the older brother he had seen only once since their father's death, remembering particularly his farewell sentence, the longest of his life, probably, compared to his usual way of making – or rather not making – conversation, out of respect for the wordless dialogue their father carried on or just through lack of interest in his own kind. Momo had never seen him get involved in arguments, not even at the peak of an election campaign; he always sat alone in his corner whenever he deigned to come out of the woods to put in an appearance at the Hôtel, which was why he'd

73

been afflicted with the nickname "The Breeze" by all of them, even though he wasn't just anybody, Momo thought, but a rare bird who had deserted the village without seeking refuge in town, something they couldn't forgive even if nobody dared reproach him openly. "A rare bird," Momo thought enviously, and as he took his cigarette out of his mouth, leaving a bit of paper stuck to his lip, he noticed his trembling hand, a sign of weakness he was quick to attribute to the cold, annoyed all the same at having been distracted from his reflections on "The Breeze" whom he now felt he could see as he was, so indifferent and above everything he didn't even look at people who tried to approach him, "maybe because he just can't take all our talk about women, our arguments about money, our gossip; that must be it; but no, maybe it ain't that neither; he was already pretty wild when he was a kid, gets it from his mother, I guess," as though he, Momo, got everything from his father, the man in the apron who was just good for doing the cooking, "too soft in the head to even hold onto his wife." Gigi appeared to him, white, her mouth open, staring accusingly. "It ain't true," he said aloud, "I ain't like him," and to prove it he moved away from the wall, opened the glass door of the restaurant and was immediately enclosed in a burst of warmth. He stuck his left hand back into the pocket of his parka. "Can you tell me if the guy with the big head..."

"Frenchy?" the waitress interrupted. "About five or ten minutes..."

She gestured to indicate that he'd left. "Funny," Momo said, "I didn't see him go." She was filling a cup with steaming coffee. Momo inhaled the good smell. "I'll have one."

"One what?" she asked, as though she'd already forgotten.

"One of those," Momo said, pointing to the cup.

"Sit yourself down at the counter if that's all you want,

because in five minutes it's gonna be full of people wanting to eat."

"How can you get out of here besides that door?" Momo asked.

She stared at him before turning her back to disappear between the tables, and Momo sat on the nearest stool, feeling the waitress's suspicious look on his back. His left hand still gripping the bone handle, he examined the large gilt-framed mirrors, the chandeliers that gave off a whitish light, the bright red moleskin seats, the pictures of Spanish scenes – a toreador taking a bull by the horns, a dancer with her skirt lifted so you could see her fine, waxy brown legs and her scarlet shoes – and he thought: "It beats the Café Central, but at home at least you can talk to people."

PART II

PART II

1

Joseph was in his rocking-chair, sucking on his big curved-stemmed pipe, his back to the counter of the general store so he could speak to the first person who came in and, if it were an old acquaintance, engage in a conversation that would be filled with allusions simply because it had been going on for decades, in spite of the frequent lack of events. He was droning on, not even caring whether he was being listened to, the same never-ending complaint about how much snow had fallen during the night, when suddenly a dark blue car came hurtling into the vacant square in front of the church; it braked so abruptly that it did a slalom across the snow and its right fender swept away a corner of the snowbank that blocked the entry to the store. Joseph got up without stopping the chair, which went on rocking by itself. "We got a visitor in a hurry this morning," he said to Phil, his only son, who was busy extricating himself from a quarter of beef that was giving him problems. Joseph stood there, his pipe between his hardened gums, trying to make out what it was that had rolled behind the man standing by the car. Twice, he raised his worn hand with its knotted joints to let the man know that he should wait, then closed it over the huge bowl of his pipe. "C'm'ere, Phil, you got a special delivery," he said finally, walking around the chair covered by a faded quilt. "What's buggin' you, pa?" Phil asked; he didn't feel obliged to take the old man's alarm seriously. "If you don't go see, I will," Joseph said, and as he stuck his head out the door he heard the man shout: "That'll teach you, you bunch of hicks!" Phil stuck his knife in the quarter of beef and went over to the door, just as the car took off again, making a U-turn in front of the church. Joseph had put on a red-and-black checked flannel shirt. "You stay here; I'll go," Phil grumbled, wiping his hands on an apron that had retained its original whiteness only around the edges. "I'm goin'!" Joseph replied, unhappy to be told to stay after he had buttoned his shirt. Phil slipped his big feet into high-heeled black leather boots, tight around the calves – boots he had long dreamed of without being able to afford them, but when he could finally buy them he was working with meat, a job he found hard to reconcile with his image of a roving cowboy, living on nothing, on horseback more often than not. But he wore them all the same, even if was just to come down from his room and go back up again after the store was closed. They were cold and wet that morning. His father opened the door, sticking his chicken's neck outside; Phil pushed him aside and went out. They could hear someone gasping, his breathing interrupted by efforts to spit. Phil jumped down the two steps, slipped and fell on his side a few steps away from Momo who was lying on his stomach and trying to lift himself up on his elbows. Phil recognized his military parka immediately, and he felt enormous beside him, "half a man," he thought, proud of his corpulence which made him appear, even in his simple butcher's clothes, twice as impressive as Momo in his lined parka. He got to his feet as though to confirm his physical superiority and roared: "Well I'll be damned, if it ain't young Boulanger!" And then, noticing the face turned towards him, he thought for a moment that he was looking at a total stranger. He heard his father say: "You gotta do something, Phil. Can't just leave the son of a bitch out there!" So there was no longer any doubt, his father wouldn't have said that about anyone but Momo, but for the time being he would help put Momo back on his feet. His face looked so appalling with its mask of beard and dried blood that Phil, who bragged about carrying quarters of beef that weighed more than Momo and "The Breeze" together, felt weak. "If them people're comin' back we're in for trouble," he said, rather reluctantly, not thinking that Momo still had the use of his ears. Joseph dropped his pipe as he yelled: "That's some cowboy!" Momo was breathing through his mouth, as though through a clogged filter. They sat him in the rocking-chair just as he was, with his blood-stained parka, hair in his eyes, his head lolling onto his shoulder as though there were nothing in his neck to support it. Joseph grimaced, distressed at the sight of the swollen lips, blood pouring slowly from them as from a spring about to dry up, but he forced himself to think: "He had it comin' to him that's for sure," because he couldn't forget the contemptuous way Gigi had treated Phil back in the days when he was chasing her, the disgusted way she had looked at his son's reddened hands, all because of that "maniac with the knife," as he called Momo, crumpled now in his own chair. "That'll show him, thinkin' he's better than the rest of us," he muttered, realizing at once that he had used almost the same expression as the man in the navy blue car, and now he didn't know which side he should be on, outraged because he'd had to swallow an insult from a stranger. "Maybe we're a bunch of hicks but we know how to live," he added, going to pick up his pipe which had fallen into the snow. Phil came over to Momo and tapped his shoulder with the air of condescending triumph of a boxer who has just knocked out his opponent in the first round. As soon as he heard his father come back he disappeared behind the counter, still wearing his boots and smiling, his face streaked with red. Deprived of his chair, Joseph walked back and forth between the displays of clothing, cans, and toys, without reaching a decision. He wouldn't have to wrack his brains too long: Ti-Pit was there, shaking the snow off his boots, wide eyed, his heavy blue canvas bag

81

swinging from his arm. "Here's the paper," he said, not really speaking to its recipient. He had recognized his cousin, a Boulanger like him, oozing blood: "Does Calixa know?"

"No, he just got here."

And the knife fell back into the meat, separating flesh from bone. Phil threw the bone into a kettle, not in the least disturbed by the event that Ti-Pit was already preparing to deliver along with the mail. "Maybe you could . . ." but Joseph didn't complete his sentence, his pipe pointing towards the west, towards the church.

"Right away," Ti-Pit agreed, "I just got time to get there."

"Maybe he won't be there," Joseph suggested.

"It's the middle of December, he oughtta be there," Ti-Pit replied, seeming sure of himself, as though he knew as much about his cousin as he did about anybody else. Then they were both silent, hesitant, occasionally darting an embarrassed look at Momo, who was sighing deeply. He was trying to speak, but his throat was filled with gurgling sounds. He was bent double, head between his knees, in an effort to empty himself of the fluid that seemed to be preventing him from breathing normally. "Hurry up and do something, you two," Joseph shouted; "don't just stand there lookin' at him!" Ti-Pit indicated that he was going and walked out, backwards, unable to turn away from Momo. Joseph came back with a glass of water which he poured over the back of Momo's neck, begging him, "Wake up, Momo," but the cold water just trickled off the bloodstained face. Joseph looked up at Phil who was bending over the counter, mouth agape: "Looks like he's bleedin' harder. Phone the doctor."

"In Laurierville?"

And as he received no reply: "We oughtta call the police."

"Just mind your own business, Phil, and call the doctor."

"What do I tell him?"

"Never mind, numskull, I'll do it."

He got up as Ti-Pit closed the door behind big Bertha whose movements were as round as she was. The wide black shawl draped over her head also served as her coat; she took it off, saying to no one in particular: "Lay him down on the floor." Ti-Pit moved first, putting an arm around Momo's waist, expecting help; Joseph seemed to be waking up. They lifted Momo out of the chair, still stiff and prostrate, then put him down on the floor where he seemed to relax at last, particularly when Bertha, ignoring the searching looks of the three silent, passive men, slipped her rolled-up shawl under his head, then asked for a clean cloth and wiped the deep cut that went from his lip to his nostril, making his dirty, bearded face unrecognizable. "He's got himself a bigger mouth," she commented, "and it's gonna take a doctor to sew it up." She got up painfully, first one leg, then the other, oblivious to the way they were looking down the front of her flowered dress, where at the slightest motion, even when she just breathed, her breasts moved; they were so heavy that when people spoke of their owner they said "Bertha's bum," a joke that Joseph had been the first to toss off in the midst of a conversation that was going around in circles. He had said precisely this: "I ran into Bertha's bum a while ago when I was leavin' our place," and the others had laughed until their bellies ached, finding it so good that they still split their sides when Joseph or someone else repeated it. Short legged, out of breath, she stared them down as she waited for they didn't know what – a word of thanks, a cup of coffee, or simply a slap on the back. "Well, what's wrong with you? Am I gonna have to phone the doctor?" It was as though Joseph were just waiting for this reminder to run for the telephone. Ti-Pit had left reluctantly, disappointed to miss what was coming, and not especially proud of the privilege of announcing the news to Calixa, thinking: "What if he just tells me to get the hell out, that whatever happens to Momo ain't none of his business?" He adjusted the strap of his bag and set off through knee-deep snow into the sparse and silent little woods behind the graveyard, taking long steps that raised great clouds of powdery snow behind him, uncertain, as he advanced, just how he was going to break the news to Calixa: "Give it to him straight or beat around the bush, it all comes down to the same thing if I know him. He won't say one goddamn word, but he's sure as hell gonna buy me a drink."

2

Ti-Pit was wiping his nose, talking through his heavy red mitten: "I never seen him get all pale like that...Didn't even finish his porridge, no kiddin'. I gave it to him straight. He stopped chewin' and his eyes was poppin' right outta his head! Didn't look like he thought it was something that could happen in any family," but Joseph cut him off, saying: "That cold fish won't even give his closest relation a hand. Goddamn savage!"

"Hell, no," Ti-Pit went on, interrupted immediately by Phil who was standing with his hands on his hips, facing the curious swarming around "like flies on a hunk of rotten meat," he said, "they think we run some kind'a hotel here and they can just walk in and see the show." Ti-Pit didn't see them; he was twisting his cap in his haste to go on without omitting a single detail, to continue the memorable story of his meeting with his cousin Calixa: "So then he tells me to go on ahead. Give him time to get here."

"So it's true, eh, Ti-Pit, you don't even have to stop for a breath when you got some hot news in your bag, eh?" Joseph said ironically; as he turned around he bumped into Bertha who was sticking close to Doctor Vachon, insisting he tell her whether the wound had been properly disinfected. "Well, you can be sure I did my best to clean it before I sewed it up," he said. His hat hung over his vast forehead when he put it on absent-mindedly, and he looked

85

at Joseph: "All right now, who's taking care of my expenses?" Bertha stared at Phil who was looking outside, while Joseph, seeming preoccupied, asked Ti-Pit when Calixa would be there. They started at the sound of a choking voice. They'd forgotten that Momo had come to: he pointed to his pants' pocket. "Come on, don't wear yourself out," Joseph said, almost paternally. Momo tried to slip his hand into the pocket which was tight against his thigh, but Bertha tapped his wrist, put her own index finger into his pocket with a grimace, and drew out a wad of bills. "Pay yourself," she said drily, as though it caused her pain. The others gathered around, expressionless. "Don't tell me you're gonna take stolen money, Doctor," Joseph insinuated. Momo hadn't stirred, he was breathing noisily, stretched out full length on the counter. The doctor unfastened the roll of money, extracted a two-dollar bill, did it up again and put it back in Momo's hand: "Better hold onto that if you want to buy yourself a steak for supper," and left with no salutation but a nod aimed at some vague target, causing Phil to say, after closing the door: "He's always been stuck-up, that one!"

"You call that stuck-up, a doctor that don't mind taking money from a thief?" Joseph asked, wounded to the core.

"Here's Calixa!" Ti-Pit announced, moving away from the door.

Bertha was the only one who noticed that Momo had closed his eyes and brought his hand nervously to his thigh just as the door opened. "*Salut*," Joseph greeted him. Phil merely nodded, needlessly as it turned out, because Calixa, without looking at them, walked over to the counter where Momo, in a deep silence broken by his breathing, had got up on his elbows, his face contorted, only his beard left as the doctor had shaved off his moustache. Calixa seemed to be attracted by the top of his swollen lip, where the sewn-up wound formed a kind of harelip; he asked in a low voice: "Can you walk?" Momo slid along the counter, still holding onto it, even after his feet were on the floor. Calixa helped him put on his parka, then, in the same silence punctuated by breathing, they went out, arms around each other's waist, both the same height, scarcely different in weight or carriage, but not walking in their usual silent, supple way because of Momo.

"Not even thanks or good day," Joseph sighed.

"Whaddya expect, pa, they ain't our kind of people," Phil replied, washing the counter where Momo had lain during the doctor's visit.

Bertha darted a quick look at them, first at Phil, then at his father, then at Ti-Pit, shrugged her shoulders, rather prim, suspecting them of running her down as cheerfully as they had done the Boulanger brothers. She wrapped her shawl around her, turned her back to them and went out, head high, nose in the air, as though she wanted to leave them with a final gesture of defiance. "Well," Ti-Pit said, "we seen everything this morning: Momo with his face all bloody, Calixa comin' out of the woods, and herself lookin' down her nose at us!"

"She still smells of hot milk," Joseph said sadly.

But Ti-Pit was already taking steps to avoid any argument, turning towards the window: "Don't that beat everything!" Joseph and Phil leaped up, each one scraping at the fine coating of frost that concealed what Ti-Pit was taking such delight in seeing, which was nothing other than Calixa kicking furiously at the door of the small house covered with brick-patterned paper, thirty yards away from the school, "if you can even call it a house," Joseph was thinking, "board walls with tin on top of them," and although he had never set foot inside he imagined it was no better there; Boulanger used to come out on the gallery to receive his rare visitors, even those who more or less regularly made him gifts of clothing or something to feed the two orphans who were just as wild as he was, never appreciating what people did to ease their bleak misery. "The poorer they are the higher they fart," he remarked in a voice that contained more than mere hostility, as though he were establishing a direct relationship between the dilapidated, practically condemned house and the brothers arrogantly breaking the glass in the door that wouldn't open. It was Momo who smashed the glass, his arm around his brother's neck. "In any case, here's what I got to say: if you want anything in this world you gotta get it yourself," Jos said, with a broad gesture towards the displays in the store for which he was only half responsible since he'd put the business into Phil's big red hands and was, himself, content to look after the inventory. He filled his pipe from the stoneware pot where he kept his tobacco, ignoring the others, nodding his head as he had got into the habit of doing as soon as he began to dream about the past or tell himself that at his age and given what he was leaving behind, he deserved to enjoy life a little; but how? "If I go chasin' after Bertha I'm gonna make a fool of myself, and anyways I ain't so sure I wouldn't just get a kick in the ass for my trouble," imagining her wielding the famous broom that she was reputed to have always within arm's reach. Just thinking about it gave him cold feet, and then his blood boiled as he remembered there had been others too, "back when she was young, in Montreal, if it's true what they say." And he drew on his pipe, his hand under his chin which was so long that people called him "Chaise-longue" behind his back, not so much out of malice as to distinguish him from the three other men in the village named Joseph.

It was past noon; the angelus had rung although no one had heard it, and Ti-Pit still hadn't finished a quarter of his rounds. He told himself that people could damn well wait: "It won't kill them if they get their Hydro bill two hours late," thus relieving his professional conscience and authorizing him to climb the scarcely cleared-off stairs to the Hôtel where there would certainly be more people curious to find out what he'd been lucky enough to see since he'd started his day, thinking too: "A little drink wouldn't be a bad thing on a day like this; never killed nobody to take his time." It wasn't the wind, the cold, or the fine powder snow that frightened him: it was having to walk all by himself for more than ten minutes without being able to open his mouth.

"It's because I ain't eaten nothing since noon yesterday," Momo said in a dull tone, through the thickness of his lip, trying again to get out of the chair whose springs stuck into his buttocks, as there was no cushion. Calixa, his back turned, motioned to indicate that he should stay there, and attached to the door the oilcloth that had always been used as a tablecloth, green oilcloth worn through to the backing at the corners, and scarred with dark rings – burns left by pots and pans. He felt as though he were seeing the table for the first time, then he vaguely made out the wood stove, flanked by a chest with one of the planks loose and hanging on by a single nail. The room seemed too big to him, cold and empty. He had to make an effort to see, on the ledge of the stove where Calixa was building a fire, the aluminum tea kettle divested of its black wooden handle, and the granite mug from which, every morning, without exception, their father used to sip his scalding tea, the tea from the night before heated up so that it had a slightly burnt taste, the taste which had always disgusted Momo so he could never drink tea, not even behind bars after he had stuffed himself with bread soaked in molasses. "It's worse than water, that garbage," but he remembered, annoyed at his brother's silence, that you could find better garbage, the proof being that he was there in the armchair, weak as a kitten, trying to reach out to Calixa who was more interested in rummaging in the stove than knowing what he'd had to put up with since they'd last seen each other. "Them bastards can make you believe anything, Calixa, and you know what the worst thing is..." His own words pounded against his temples, and he told himself: "Don't yell, come on, talk like a normal person," then continued almost softly, hoping that Calixa could still hear a little of what he was trying to explain in spite of the racket he was making as he poked at the fire: "When I saw she was dead I didn't touch

89

nothing, not even my knife. I couldn't....When I got outside I thought about what I oughtta do: get the hell out or find out what was goin' on. Once, I nearly got on the bus, but then I thought, no, that's just what them bastards want. So I hung around the whole blessed day, till I didn't know if I oughtta stay or go. It got dark early. And all that time, after Frenchy did his disappearing act from the restaurant, I told myself I was gonna run into him at the Paradise. I got there first, you better believe it. Not a soul, just the people that work there. Then all of a sudden I see Frenchy and I go chasin' after him. And that's when they got me – it was just me against the three of them. The second time it happened! Besides trying to pass me off as a killer they had to mess up my face. Did you see that?" He smiled, or tried to, as much as his sutured lip would allow him, but he felt a sudden urge to whimper, to burst into sobs or cries while Calixa was emptying the coffee-pot into the tea-kettle, forgetting that there was no running water in the house, or electricity, since Momo had stopped paying the bills. He got up, elbows on his knees, head down: "But I know one person that's gonna have a scar somewhere, as long as he lives, because I gave him a good one before they laid me out, in the arm I think it was, anyway he yelled like a stuck pig. The rest of them stopped laughing. I don't really know what happened afterwards, I got one of their feet right in the face. When I woke up it hurt everywhere, especially there," and he pointed to his lip and behind it where several teeth were missing, gesturing to Calixa to come closer: "Here, Calixa, come and take a look." He had shouted and blood was pouring into his throat, warm and salty, thick as pea soup, and into his beard. He lifted his lip with his finger and Calixa squinted, still holding the tea-kettle, standing there in his green-and-black checked shirt, "worn right down to the bare threads since he's been wearing it with nothing on under it, even in the winter," Momo thought, a little ashamed at having shouted, but relieved too to see him so close, his skin brown and glistening, like a horse. He

90

laughed deep in his throat, hollowly: "You're no better'n me, you leave marks on your underwear, don't try and tell me any different! Did you know our own mother spent her life in a mud hut? If you don't, you're the only one. Even them fucking bastards in town know we're Indian brats." Calixa still hadn't moved. Momo only heard him say: "Say that again and I'll smash your face in!" Momo laughed: "As if it wasn't busted up enough already." Calixa wasn't laughing, he never laughed or smiled or whistled a tune, satisfied just to be there without really being there, a simple passer-by anxious to be done with other people's stories, "it's no skin off his ass what happens to me," Momo thought, "as long as he's alone in his woods with his gun and enough *caribou* so it don't freeze between his legs, I matter as much to him as that there plaster statue," perched in the corner of the opposite wall for as long as he could remember, in her sky-blue gown which clashed with the rough wood of the walls that had stayed as they were, with no other ornament, while everywhere else, in any house you could think of, even Phonse's, there were family pictures, calendars, knick-knacks. And now Calixa put on his red hunting jacket and went out, saying: "Stay there, I'll be back," and he felt lost in the deserted house, hearing the oil-cloth rustle against the broken glass, imagining what was surely going to happen any minute now – the goose-shit coloured provincial police car, the handcuffs, the questions; they'd take off his belt, his shoelaces; and then the long corridors, the cell, meals in common till he died, preferring to rot in his hole instead of working; but since Reddy was dead what was he going to think about, locked up all day long? It was as though he were stumbling into the void with nothing to hang onto. He took a few steps, then leaned on the table, thinking: "I know what they're gonna say if I run away, they're gonna say that Mo's a shit. Enough of the old man in him, that old woman that wasn't good for nothing but making stew out of the neighbours' leftovers. I can't take it..." He got up and went to the cabinet with one of its

doors gaping open, dangling from a single hinge. He picked
up the double-barrelled 410, hefted it, "If I sawed off the
end I could make it into something pretty good," but his
voice was quavering in a kind of nervous jubilation. Some
cartridges rolled along the shelf; he picked up a handful
and stuffed them in the pocket of his parka. He was shivering. But ten minutes later when the door opened he was
soaking wet. Calixa didn't even look at him. He put his
khaki-coloured canvas bag on the floor, stuffed some wood
in the stove and held out a "naked" flask, one without a
commercial label. "Drink that while I heat up the beans,"
he said, not seeming to notice the rifle Momo was hacking
at with an old iron saw. Momo sniffed at the warm smells;
unable to put the neck of the flask between his lips he
poured some of the pinkish liquid, a mixture of cherry wine
and alcohol, into the hollow of his hand, kept it in his
mouth for a moment, just long enough to rinse his gums;
then he spat it out, poured a second portion and this time
swallowed it in one gulp, gasping, waiting for the heat to
rise from his stomach and spread through his body. He
went back to sawing with his left hand, sniffing all the time.

The pork and beans must have been on the point of sticking to the bottom of the pan, judging by the burned smell,
stronger than the smell of hot metal, that reminded him of
how their father, who had gone deaf and dumb the day his
wife took off, would sit in front of the stove, forgetting to
take the shepherd's pie or beef stew out of the oven. And
now the house was inhabited by a slow, tepid kind of life
again that spread into the slightest sound – the plank that
went across the kitchen and cracked along its whole length
under the weight of a foot or the rocking-chair, the resin
crackling in the stove like gunshots, the saucepan where
thin slices of potatoes were sizzling along with pork or beef
sausages, "I've had my fill of that in my life, sausages that
was just going bad that Chaise-longue wouldn't dare sell to
nobody else and my father cooked them till they were worse
than charcoal; and when I think that Reddy wanted to

make me eat them that time I took her into the cornfield."
He felt a lump in his throat, as though the memory were an
invisible and vengeful hand that clutched him without his
knowledge, forcing him to open his eyes and see Gigi, so
young then, so warm, lips rather pale, the colour of veal,
finely striated lips that provoked desire. He told himself she
didn't know how to do it back then, any more than he did,
in fact – inveterate virgin, content to rub himself against
maple trees, their still-smooth bark, or sprawl in velvety
beds of pine needles; so many nights spent dreaming of her,
so much accumulated desire, that he didn't want to miss
this opportunity to be swallowed raw between the thighs of
a real woman; but in the end it was she who had held him,
scratching his back and grimacing with pleasure or pain,
while he insisted that she swear fidelity to him before he
consummated his pleasure, perhaps to give that moment a
taste of eternity.

He gulped down some more *caribou*, furious at his heart
pounding with desire for her, though she was well and truly
dead, and wondering how he could have wanted her, sleeping in the big bed that other men had warmed, making him
forget his internment when he had been nothing but a vegetable, prisoner of his memories; his desire was stronger than
hunger or fear, although his disgust had prevented him
from getting it up like the first man who arrived with fifteen or twenty dollars to put on the little varnished night-
table. "Talk about a pig, gets me put away so she can take
off with a pimp that stinks of garlic and then the bastard
gets rid of her; but worst of all, I'll be the one that pays if I
don't get my hands on the guy that did it"; then, seeing
that Calixa was barely listening to him, behind the smoke
of his short clay pipe, no more party to it all than the plaster Virgin who had stood there in her corner since the
beginning of eternity, hands clasped on her star-covered
sky-blue gown, slightly yellowed by time and heat, Momo
was silent and kicked at the back of the chair, splitting the
worn plush stretched tight as the skin of a drum. Then he

braced his foot on the shotgun lying across the arms of the chair, took off his parka which he didn't need now that the house was warming up and the alcohol circulating in his veins, and he listened to his stomach which was emptying itself, sounding like a sewer pipe. The fine teeth barely bit into the gun barrel, sprinkling his hand with a fine coating of grey dust. The board creaked all along its length. Calixa put the can of beans boiling in their juice – a mixture of grease and molasses – on the table. "Come on and eat," he said.

"You could'a told me before."

"Suit yourself," Calixa replied, his legs crossed on the edge of the big square table that looked strange now without the oilcloth, which was crackling in the wind. The day was growing dim, barely lighting the windows, and Momo stuck his eye against the narrow slit that shortened the barrel by at least seven inches. His forearm was stiffened by a cramp. "You take over while I have something to eat." Calixa took his feet off the table, came over to the chair without stepping on the board that creaked and moved the rifle so he could saw with his right hand. Momo took a good swig of *caribou* and caught his breath; there was some of it in his beard. Calixa lit the lamp and hung it on a nail. Momo watched him peacefully sawing with slow, regular movements, wondering whether he'd go to the Paradise with him, as he'd made every effort to believe until Calixa threatened to smash his face. Just then Calixa stopped to look at him, his long black eyes half shut under lowered lids: "Know what I'd do? I'd leave the gun here and go and see the inspector." Momo kept chewing the forkful of beans he had just put into his mouth, rather painfully, staring at his brother who seemed to be waiting for an answer, holding the sawed-off gun. They stayed like that for a moment, silent, each one surprised at having thought of the same thing in such a contradictory manner. "If that's the way it is," Momo said at last, "I'll handle it myself," adding a few seconds later, "Just like I always done, eh?" Calixa shook his pipe against the arm of the chair. Momo almost knocked his own chair over when he heard a knock at the door. He grabbed the gun from Calixa and stuck two cartridges into the breech while Calixa went slowly to the door; it opened before he had even lifted the oilcloth. Marie-Rose was holding onto the door when she saw Momo, clutching the gun in both hands and aiming it at her; his face was contorted by the soft, intermittent light of the lantern, almost grimacing with the effort to repeat the same curse, a little louder each time. He lowered the hammer of the gun. Her hair had come undone and was hanging between her neck and her white leather collar. She was trying to get her breath back, mouth open, nostrils quivering, and he looked at her as though she were the cause of all his problems. "Don't stay here, Momo. Phonse said he was gonna get you, that's what Phil told me. I just had time to put on my coat and come and warn you. Come on," and she held out her keychain. "Nobody'll guess you're at our place. My God, what happened to you?" she asked, and Momo was too stupefied to answer her or to reach for the keys. "I gotta go before Paul starts wonderin' where I am," then she turned, the stiff, cheap leather coat making a dry sound, and disappeared as quickly as she'd come. Calixa kept looking down at the bowl of his pipe which hung from his teeth. "I don't get none of the breaks," Momo said, "now here I am with that idiot on my tail." Calixa drew on his pipe, which had gone out, his back against the stove, saying in his usual low voice, without intonation: "If you wanta make trouble, Maurice, it's your business, but don't count on me. Do like I say and go and see the inspector." Momo turned around, brandishing the 410: "Get moving, and fast!" And as Calixa was putting on his jacket, he strode up to him. "You're shivering," Calixa remarked without the slightest irony, in that tone of his that Momo detested but imitated constantly; it wasn't just the tone of voice that got on his nerves, but the air of detachment, "as if he knows more than anybody else." He

envied that most of all: the animal strength that allowed
Calixa to live as he wished, not even prizing life itself or
anything else. As Calixa was closing the door Momo
shouted, index finger stiff on the trigger: "That's right, you
shit, go and hide!" He lifted the oilcloth that covered the
window. "Hey Calixa! Whadda I owe you?" But there was
no answer. Calixa was walking with his peaceful animal's
gait, stubborn and solitary, leaving regular, evenly spaced
prints in the snow behind him, walking away as straightfor-
ward and determined as that day in October or November
when he'd left the house, never to set foot in it again except
to bring back their father's frozen body. Momo strained to
follow him in the darkness that buried every footstep.
"Maybe we won't ever see each other again," he thought,
letting go of the oilcloth which dropped as though it were
melting. He was annoyed at himself for being so scared in
front of Marie-Rose, scared enough to tremble like a leaf
even after she'd gone; and he was still scared, his nerves in a
knot, knowing nothing could deliver him now that he was
alone and didn't dare leave the house. "It's because of that
gun," he thought, and to test it he aimed at the Blessed Virgin perched on her shelf in the corner and fired. Practically
nothing in the shoulder, hardly any pressure even, but he
was astonished at the uproar he had caused. The boards
were pitted with shot; the statue had fallen off, decapitated,
the blue gown marked with whitish streaks. "It gives off a
hell of a charge. I feel sorry for any asshole that sticks his
face in front of that," he said as he reloaded the smoking
barrel. The acrid smell of powder made him sniff. But he
was breathing easier now. A windowpane had shattered
and the cold was coming in. He nailed a grey blanket to the
window frame and then, having discovered some candles,
he stuck one in a saucepan and lit it, and blew out the lamp
whose flame was now nothing but a sputter of sparks. He
pushed the chest in front of the door, moved the enormous
cushionless armchair between the stove and the door, put a
birch log in the stove, and stationed himself behind the

door with the gun, the pot with the burning candle, an incomplete deck of cards, and sat on his rolled-up parka. He would have liked to drink something besides Calixa's alcohol or at least to cut it with water. He ate a few spoonfuls of cold beans to stave off his desire for a smoke.

Headlights lit the opposite wall, then nothing. The roar of the fire. The persistent musty smell and the oilcloth flapping against the chest. He told himself that Phonse had never held anything in his hands except his reins, "his reins and his hunting rifle," adding, "when he could still use one," although he didn't feel reassured. "He must'a figured I'm the one that done it, but I'd swear on a stack of bibles, he thinks he's gonna have the fun of shooting me in the back." He started. But it was only the log bursting in the stove.

3

He ran his fingers through his beard, which was wet with saliva and lifted his head; his neck felt broken and he was furious that he'd fallen asleep that way, defencelessly, leaving himself open to attack, for an hour or maybe longer, no way to know, he'd always had only a very rough idea of time, and as he groped around in the dark his foot struck something that clanked, "the kettle," he thought, and his heart stopped. He could hear nothing but his rapid breathing. His throat was tickling. "Take it easy," he told himself as he sat down again, his back against the wall, which felt indifferent, neither warm nor cold, a simple spruce-wood partition covered with the tarred paper which served as insulation between the wood and the sand-coated paper made to look like brick that had never been changed since the house was built in the twenties, when old Boulanger had abandoned his rocky land. "What an idea that was, wantin' to grow vegetables in the middle of the woods, in the rocks," Momo thought; the grandfather, still smelling of the soil, had opened a barber shop, quite an innovation in a village where the housewife always cut her family's hair, free, after Mass and the Sunday roast. The old man had a huge white moustache, yellowing at the corners of the lips, and a crackling straw hat he took off only when he sat down at the table or went to bed.

After he found his gun his breathing slowed down and the only thing that bothered him was his craving for a smoke, even a pipe, he missed it so much. He struck a match on the floor and, cupping it in his hand to hide the flame, he bent over double and ran to the chest where he found a few candle stubs which he put back, alarmed at a creaking sound coming from outside – the steps that were half rotten but solidified by the cold – then he thought he heard someone breathing. Someone who had been running. He moved the oilcloth aside with the tip of his gun, asking in a voice so feeble that it startled him: "Who's there?"

"Me."

"Hang on."

And he pushed aside the chest that was blocking the door. Without even giving him time to replace the barricade Marie-Rose grabbed his shoulder: "Don't stick around here, Momo. Come over to our place."

"Not so loud," he said, standing with his back against the chest.

"I went home for nothing. You weren't there and I didn't have my keys neither."

"There they are," Momo replied, striking a match to light a candle, its short wick drowning immediately in the melted wax. The match flame burned his thumb. Marie-Rose flicked on her silver lighter and he lit the candle again and stuck it into the puddle of hardened wax in the bottom of the pot. He sat down and looked at her: "Cigarette." She held out her package, then slumped into the armchair, facing him as he savoured his first cigarette of the day, although his swollen lips made it hard to smoke. "It's freezing in here," she said finally, as though to justify her presence. "All you gotta do is put some wood in the stove." She did so, rubbing her hands over the fire. Then she rummaged in her purse and took out a cellophane-wrapped sandwich. "I forgot your coffee," she confessed with an embarrassed smile. He put out what was left of his cigarette and when he tried to bite into the ham sandwich it revived the pain in his gums. He tore at the ham, swallowing it without chewing. "I feel better already," he said, his hand on the cold flask. Then, not looking at him, sitting very close, she said, "Momo, if you was smart you'd come over to our place. Ma's in the hospital and I'm all by myself." His reply was a belch. She was fiddling with her lighter, flicking it on absent-mindedly, when Momo's hand came down on her wrist so abruptly that the lighter slipped between the folds of her coat and was lost somewhere in her skirt; he began to search without realizing that her silence, her immobility and her abandon were laden with desire. Even the fact that she had spread her legs didn't surprise him – he confused the movement with his search for the lighter, a love present from Phil, he assumed. He shuddered when he touched the warm skin of her thigh, but pretended he was still looking for the lighter which had become just a pretext: with bowed head, he looked at her rounded knee, her long thigh glowing in the pale and trembling candlelight; then the blood boiled in his flesh and he had a sneezing fit, sprinkling Marie-Rose's thighs, so that she burst out laughing and buried her head in the hollow of his shoulder. He let her cling to him until she opened her mouth to say: "Poor Momo, you oughtta come over to our place." Then he wrapped her hair around his hand and pushed her head back without making her lower the eyes that were staring at him with a kind of joyful insolence: "Don't ever call me poor Momo, you hear me!" She grimaced, showing her small teeth, almost square and widely spaced. He pulled her hair a little and she fell back, a shoulder emerging from the cold white coat he helped her to take off, moved by the warmth of her body under the thin sweater. She closed her eyes as he rubbed her shoulder, his knee between her closed legs. "Take your boots off," he ordered, his arm stretched out to pick up the flask which he had kicked over. She took off one boot. He held the flask out to her and lay on his side, rolling down the white stocking that came up to her thigh, so light in his hand that he thought of Gigi's, twice as broad or so it seemed; and her small foot, narrow in spite of the toes spread like a fan, like the webbed foot of a frog, stayed in his hand motionless, warm and fragrant, with a life of its own like a sluggish beast. Bending over it he forgot the other foot, still in its boot, and when she held her arms out to him he knelt between her legs, trembling, his fingertips grazing the slight swelling in her damp pink underpants. He slipped his hands awkwardly under her buttocks and pulled the pants down onto her thighs, then he lowered his head. She closed her thighs, holding him there, and her pleasure at imprisoning him was spoiled a little by the tenacious fear that she was committing an irreparable act, although she was in no hurry to free him from this position, an unfamiliar one for her and all the more pleasant because there was no risk involved; eyes closed, feeling her belly stir, she abandoned herself to what she had always refused, to him as to others, believing that her virginity was the only thing special about her, her only power over men and her own future. Suddenly, with no warning, while she was thinking of the long evenings when Phil went so far as to crush her breasts in his rough red hands, breathing like an ox, there was an unbearable void in the place where, a little earlier, there had been all that she could ask of life, and she let out a cry of surprise as she opened her flesh to him and he gradually entered her, as though it were her own flesh swelling, an overflowing of herself that made her insensitive to everything else, to fear, to the cold air coming between the floor boards and even to the pain which grew more intense as he pushed inside her. Momo didn't kiss her but kept his face buried in her hair, his left hand on her breast which was no bigger than an orange; then he stopped moving, thinking she was crying, but began again to probe inside her when he felt her fingernails digging into his back. She was whimpering now, like a puppy, but it didn't matter to him, squeezed as he was in a knot from which he felt it was impossible to disengage himself, at least as long as his penis was an excessive extension of himself – and also as

101

long as his male vanity had not obtained its legitimate satisfaction by breaking her virgin's web. He no longer heard her moans, only the sound of his own boots scraping along the floor and the sort of harsh groan from the belly, as urgent as a hiccup, when the web gave way and he sank to the root in the warmth of her muscles and blood, thinking only, "too bad, but I couldn't stop," as though nothing else mattered now. And then the dark night, and the salvation of sex, and he swept down on her, still shaken by convulsive movements it pleased him to bring on by pushing his penis inside her, nearly exhausted now, just stiff enough to record the palpitations of the knot of muscles, viscous now, which he was in no hurry to leave, although he was already certain he would soon be rejected like a dead fish, expelled from the salutary bite, thinking it was different with Gigi because then he had galloped through something that resembled a thick, oily night, without this feeling of profound immersion in the most vital part of her flesh; but the galloping would come to an abrupt end when for no reason Gigi either began to laugh like a horse neighing, or talk to him, for example, about Phil's brand-new truck, hinting that she just had to say the word and he'd give her the moon. "It was always like that," he thought, but he remembered that no, not the first time, when she had gripped his shoulders and refused to swear. The other times she did it just to please him, indifferent even when he could feel her being carried away in the thick, slippery tide. He put his hand on Marie-Rose's thin shoulder as she purred against him, and tried to say, "I didn't know . . ." Her pale, angular face was turned to him: "Wanta go to our place?" Her small wet eyes shone like pavement. He moved away abruptly. "Goddamn women! We always gotta be following you someplace and our pockets gotta be full too, otherwise it don't work, right?" He got up, the flask gurgling into his wide open mouth. There was a burst of crackling and she cried out. Momo laughed: "Scaredy cat!" She was sitting with her hands on her knees. "If anybody found out, a nice girl like you with a murderer like me . . ." Barely visible in the feeble light coming from the kettle, she opened her arms, but he preferred to sit withdrawn, slightly behind her, so he could enjoy the breast which from his vantage point looked conical, accentuated by the protuberance of the nipple pointing to the line of her legs that dwindled down to the narrow foot on her flattened boot. He gulped down some more alcohol, almost choked, offered her the cold flask. Then he lit a cigarette in the candle flame. Marie-Rose spat out the small amount of alcohol she had taken in. "You're wasting it," he said, closing the flask. She was stretched out beside him, her cheek against his belly, laughing as she listened to the stomach noises that indicated the intense fermentation of the alcohol. "Pretty noisy down there," she said, tapping him on the belly, while he felt the pulse beating in the vein of his neck and told himself it was good to be plugged into someone else's life this way. "Hey, what if Phil saw us, eh? I bet he'd have a stroke. Sometimes big guys with red faces like that just drop dead, you know, just like that. You're gonna have to look after him." Then he was silent. She spoke against the wall of his abdominal muscles, almost on the verge of tears: "Whose fault is it, Momo? I tried to talk to you, but you wouldn't even listen to me. There was just Gigi, nobody else. I didn't matter any more than a chair or a table or..."

"How was I supposed to know?"

"Do you think I'm gonna go and ruin my whole life now?"

"I didn't ask you for nothing," he said, amazed that it had even occurred to her, adding immediately: "It's too late." And she asked, sitting astride him now, "Why'd you do it?"

"Even if I didn't do nothing there's no way I can prove it. Nobody was at her place except big Gène."

"Gène?"

"A customer," he said, bursting out laughing.

"So it was true, what everybody was saying."

103

He was silent. "Gigi went that far?" He swung her onto her side, furious: "When a girl's in the city with a pimp whaddya think she does, eh? She's gotta give the assholes that come to see her more than a cup of coffee!" She looked down: "You had a good reason..."

"To kill her?"

"That isn't what I meant."

"Same thing."

She spoke very softly: "You're really hard on women." He dug his fingers into her shoulder, not realizing she was gritting her teeth: "That's what everybody thinks, eh?" She snuggled up to him, shaking her head against the hollow of his shoulder: "I'm cold, Momo." His fingers were wet as he moved his hand over her cheek. "Go to sleep," he said, covering her with his parka. "Where you going?" He listened to the wind sighing in the chimney. "Up north. As far as I can go; I don't know. I don't even know if I'm going away."

"I'm scared."

"Don't think about it no more. Go to sleep."

But he stayed where he was, leaning over her and shivering, his arm held out to the rifle he kept within reach, thinking he'd have peace until morning at least, that if the police had been warned they didn't seem too anxious to find him. Who wanted to get him arrested before Phonse had the chance to carry out his own form of justice? "Likely that's what they're waiting for, the bastards. Phonse must'a told them: You'll see what's gonna happen," he thought, without feeling any fear, almost relieved in fact to imagine them – the village and Phonse – accomplices in their need to avenge Gigi. But they could always come, they'd find their Marie-Rose asleep in his parka and in the lingering odour of love. He raised the hammer on his gun, then lowered it. A long moment of silence had separated him from Marie-Rose, whose eyelashes were rubbing against the sleeve of his sweater. He bent over to close her eyes with his lips. His tongue felt the salty taste of tears. A good swig of *caribou* would drown the bitter taste. He got up, ears buzz-

104

ing, wondering why he was so sensitive to alcohol, and this time he sat in the armchair where he could see the bright sky and the white snow, apparently so immutable that he felt as though he were living in a kind of eternity stripped of all movement, as though time, the world, and life were fixed once and for all, condemning him to an endless agony as well. When he raised his hand to blur this vision he felt it trembling uncontrollably. With his head flung back on the chair, the gun between his legs, "like pa that day when Calixa found him as stiff as a fence post," he tried to keep his eyes open in spite of the fatigue weighing down his eyelids. They were already drooping when he stopped staring at the ceiling; it was dark, and he descended, projected into the void, slowly at first, then faster and faster, until the nape of his neck struck against the floor of a cell, and he felt a painful smarting sensation all through his body – Frenchy's enormous fist making his teeth crack in his gums; then, not realizing what had happened in the meantime, he found himself lying flat on his belly in the alley, his mouth filled with dirty snow, looking at Nico who was still leaning against the frame of the emergency exit. Their jerky laughter was amplified by the intolerable pain bursting in his head. He had managed to get back on his feet when Vic pushed him over towards someone he didn't know, a tall wiry guy who punched him in the stomach – and he couldn't dodge the blow or even protect himself, as though Frenchy's punch had paralysed him. Nico left then, he assumed, satisfied with the way things were going, abandoning him to the others who hadn't had enough, who were playing with him as though he were a balloon, laughing when he staggered and collapsed, his face in the stinking snow. And then he ran out of the strength, or the courage, to get up again. Frenchy was laughing loud above him as he knelt, knees soaked, dazed and panting. He heard a door open, Nico's strident voice shouting: "Hurry up, you guys, get outta here. Take him back home." He thought he was really going to get a taste of it now. Only that, without thinking any further. His hand squeezed the bone handle. And when the shadow approached him on his left, he threw himself on it with all his weight. A scream followed the comforting sensation of a conquered obstacle, his knife stuck into something hard – a short-lived pleasure because immediately, or almost, his head exploded. And when he came to, in the slowly moving car, he had noticed only one thing, the intense burning of his lip and nose, and he thought: "That's it, they're takin' me back there," the same isolated prison on that treeless plain, the same cell where he'd wait for the time to pass, for his time to be served; but if it was happening again, he thought, the time wouldn't pass, he'd never get out, even though the judge hadn't sentenced him yet because for the moment he was wedged in between two guards, unable to say a single word to defend himself, with the cut that burned right through his lip and the blood that kept running into his beard, turning cold before it dried, blood as bright as Gigi's when she was lying on the stretcher, testifying against him, showing her back – the knife stuck in it, the knife he had weighed in his hands so many times before throwing it into the wall, a good knife that clicked when you pressed the button and its blade sprang out as fast as a snake's tongue. The car skidded during a turn, then started moving normally again. He opened his eyes and saw not the court, the judge, Gigi's back, but the church and the houses of Laurierville moving past him so that they looked piled up on one another, then the hardware store he had robbed and the dark spruce trees on the white horizon. An abrupt stop threw him forward, his head against his knees. He could barely see the sign pointing to Saint-Emmanuel, the cottages around the artificial lake; he closed his eyes again, tossed about by the hurtling of the overheated car, choking in the cigar smoke, remembering the blow he had inflicted but unable to understand that the night had passed without him. A damp hand forced him to his feet. He continued to play dead. He recognized the driver – it was Vic – by the wavy hair that came down his neck and by the way his ears stuck out. He wanted to get his arm out from under Frenchy's weight; he just looked at the stranger he had wounded the night before out of the corner of his eye. The pale, hollow face was made uglier by long teeth that kept his mouth open, as though he couldn't get rid of a big candy. He was looking straight ahead, holding a cigar, his hand on his knee. The smoke burned Momo's eyes and he wondered where the four of them were going: certainly not to the police station – to his place, rather, to the village where no one was expecting him, not even his own brother. "What's wrong with them?" he kept thinking. They were going to knock him out once they got there, in front of everybody, and go away laughing like madmen! He could already see himself frozen stiff like his father, losing blood, waiting for Calixa to take him back to the house so that he could die in peace at least, warm and sheltered from the wind. The village swooped down on them, after the first turn and the Texaco station; he could recognize every house now, most of them white under their tin roofs. The tall wiry one stuck his cigar between his protruding teeth and held out his arm to shake Frenchy who started sending his own elbow into the tall one's jaw. "Stop!" Frenchy shouted, and Momo closed his eyes, his right arm free now of Frenchy's weight as Frenchy pushed the door open. The wiry one started pushing Momo out the door and Frenchy dragged him out by the hair. He rolled onto the fresh snow, heard a door creak and Frenchy shout, "That'll teach you, you goddamn bunch of hicks, think you're better than the rest of us!" The car made a U-turn, he saw Phil, immense in his black boots, with his bloated face, and then Joseph's wrinkled features, his big pipe dangling from his lips.

4

The snow looked pink in the dawn. And the face of the sleeping girl as he looked at her, clenching his fists, was pink too. He had the strange sensation that the skin had shrunk on his flesh, like when he drank. He moved his joints, the gun squeezed between his ribs and elbow. The floor board creaked, but Marie-Rose still slept, her arms folded on the parka wrapped around her waist. As he looked at her pale face in the pink rays of morning he imagined her being held by "that pig Phil," and he muttered, "if I'd'a known," one knee on the floor, his hand trembling above the narrow white foot which he did not even touch with his fingertips, at least until its cold made him start and say very softly: "I can't just go away like that, without saying nothing." He wanted to free her from the sleeve of the parka which was twisted around her legs. She sighed as she buried her face in the imitation fur lining. He got up, shivering, and poured the rest of the alcohol from the flask into the granite mug. He swallowed and it trickled down his throat, cold and harsh. Then he waited for the alcohol to explode and spread through his limbs like healing oil, staring at the plaster statue which had moved, swinging as it slipped from its modest pedestal, just a hunk of wood, not even painted or varnished, that seemed to have lost all its power – if it had ever had any – over any person or thing. At any rate he had never paid it the slightest attention, perhaps because his father used to glance at it as he drank his tea, glances that went on forever, as though the plaster statue were more important than his own children; they were just tossed in with the other household objects that interfered with or broke into the perpetual meditation that was more than a refuge, a reason for remaining patient, for going on until the day when the mystery his wife had taken with her when she disappeared after only two years of life together would finally be revealed to him. Smiling in spite of the stitches that shrank his lip which was less swollen now than the day before, Momo exclaimed: "Poor Ma Boulanger!" And he was suddenly filled with pity for the man whose expression, like that of a beaten dog, had for twenty years looked imploringly at a figure now riddled with whitish holes.

Marie-Rose moved. He opened the doors of the cupboard revealing the jumble of faded clothes his father had worn before giving them to him. He put on a flannel shirt with only one button, then a long blackish-green wool jacket, too tight around the shoulders, that gave off a smell of grease and damp, very different from the spicy smell of burned wood and resin impregnating Calixa's heavy checked wool shirt, Calixa whom he would probably never see again because he was leaving for the North, a lifetime away from what had been his life until then – his work at the sawmill, now in ruins with its piles of greying timber and its mound of sawdust turned hard as cement, and his traps in the woods. Now he was the one who was going to run, disoriented like a panic-stricken beast, just because one summer Sunday he had taken Gigi into a cornfield.

He moved the chest and opened the door to a gust of wind that took his breath away. Turning his back to the west, where the wind was coming from, he threw back his head to gargle with the last mouthful of alcohol. The red sky dazzled him. He lowered his eyes after throwing the mug to the other end of the gallery and it seemed as though the snow was on fire, the earth incandescent; then he urinated for a long time, a honeyed stream that sputtered in

109

the snow as it hollowed out a hole. He was holding the gun, so cold that his finger stuck to the trigger. The snow's brightness forced him to close his eyes. A motor roared, drawing his attention to the side of the road that went down to the village. Squinting, he tried to see what could be on the mountain road so early in the morning, a road that was rarely travelled in the middle of winter. The car slid along the layer of windswept snow. The motor roared and he noticed the red flasher on the roof of the car. He jumped over the gallery railing and, in spite of the softness of the snow, headed for the spruce grove a hundred feet from the house. As he was leaning against a trunk to catch his breath a detonation in the clear, still air made him spin around. The gun jumped from his hand and landed in the snow. He lay on his stomach, feeling nothing but a heaviness in his shoulder, as though his arm were detached from his body. The car stopped in the middle of the road. The man in the Tyrolean hat hesitated, standing with his arms dangling at the sides of his grey tweed coat.

Inspector Therrien looked like a lost traveller, pensive and undecided. He turned his head in the direction of the house which leaned slightly towards the village, went over to the distraught young woman wearing nothing but a sweater, her bare foot scarcely touching the rotten wood of the steps. He took off his hat in a gesture that could pass for a greeting and said very softly: "If I were you I'd take a minute to put my shoes on. Summer's been over for two or three months now." And repeating the same gesture – the right hand lifting the hat – he signalled to the driver of the car and, taking long strides as though trying to avoid wetting his feet, he went over to the dark stain on the snow at the edge of the woods, followed by Marie-Rose who gasped each time she stuck her bare leg into the snow. "If she insists on seeing it," the inspector muttered, "she's going to see it all right." The tuft of black hair came closer. He stopped, out of breath, to reproach her, but his voice was hardly convincing: "Did I ask you for anything?" She stared him

110

down, her face drained of colour, fists clenched on her belly. Then she raised her bare leg which was red all the way to the thigh. He held out his hand in its black wool glove and she clutched it, walking more slowly.

They heard a harsh, quavering murmur. He had expected her to throw herself onto the body, the neck turned up to the sky, but no, not the slightest movement aside from the hand squeezing his arm, squeezing then releasing him, and her plea: "Do something! Don't just stand there and stare at him." His hand skimmed the narrow-brimmed, featherless hat, rapidly this time, and he shook his arm to release the hand that was crushing his wrist. As he bent over the face half-buried in the snow, he could see Momo grimace, his mouth opening and closing like a fish's, as though he were trying to say the only thing that could matter for him now. Blood glistened in the dark opening fringed with ravelled wool between his shoulder and throat. "The bullet must've gone out," he thought, not daring to lift Momo's arm. "If you want to do something," he said to Marie-Rose who was kneeling behind him, hands on her knees, "go tell the driver to come back here with Florent Dupré, fast. And put some clothes on while you're at it." But she didn't seem inclined to move, despite the prickling sensation beneath her skin and the fact that she could do nothing better than run and give the driver the inspector's message. He had to lift her up and remind her she might catch her death. That expression, which he regretted as soon as he had uttered it, had the effect of a slap, and she ran towards the house, arms whirling. He unbuttoned his coat, after taking the glove off his right hand, and stared for a moment at the stub of the cigar he had lit very early that morning and which had gone out somewhere along the way. He stuck it into the corner of his mouth absent-mindedly, as though there were an orifice planned for that very purpose, no larger than the one from which Momo's blood was flowing peacefully. He kept his hand on Momo's arm and neglected to light his cigar. He got to his feet with a

111

sigh, not even glancing at Momo, and moved away. "What else can I do?" he asked himself, annoyed that they had pulled the rug from under his feet when he had just come to handcuff Momo, thinking he'd have to worm the information out of Phonse who had not only squealed on Momo and sent him behind bars for almost two years, but had probably allowed himself the luxury of self-justification by saying that everybody would be on his side, blaming Momo and supporting him for avenging his daughter. "This is some business!" he said loud enough to be heard, as though he wanted Momo to explain why he'd thought he could save his skin by hiding out in his father's house, "and with a girl into the bargain." Then he bent down to pick up the butt of the 410 stuck in the snow and stood there motionless, holding the rifle until the arrival of the Mayor-Funeral Director and Fred, a giant who acted mainly as a chauffeur and to whom he said as little as possible for fear of giving him the excuse to smash down doors. "That youngster's too keen," he thought as Fred made the snow fly in front of the stretcher he was carrying, hands behind his back, sinking into the snow, then coming out of it and puffing like an engine. Dupré coughed to indicate his presence to the inspector who was lost in the rumination that made him, in the opinion of the village at least, a good sort who didn't really belong in the police, with his bland face, his greying moustache that dipped down over his lip and the inevitable cigar in the corner of his mouth that left a depression when he took it out. What fascinated Dupré was not just the inspector's absent, unconcerned manner, but his skill at talking without moving the cigar, which always stayed in place as though welded there, in a corner of flesh become paralysed while the lips moved with great ease. Dupré jerked his head when he heard Momo gasp, seeming to note a fact he had long predicted and placed in the category of fate. Slightly smaller than Fred, built on the same lines as the former wrestler Johnny Rougeau – a resemblance he was proud of – Dupré liked to let people know what he

112

thought just by gestures so that no one – especially his wife – ever knew what was really going on in his head; his muteness was sufficiently ambiguous to assure him a sort of permanence in the mayor's office. "Everything okay with you, Mr. Mayor?" the inspector asked. Florent shook his head from left to right, indolently, indicating that this business embarrassed him greatly. "It isn't the kind of publicity, you understand..." For a moment the inspector had the illusion that he would complete the sentence. "Gotta do this fast," the inspector said: "Fred, you go along with the ambulance. And don't forget, remember anything Boulanger might have to say. Get it down on paper, it's safer." Fred nibbled the tip of his moustache, moving his big hands over his goose-shit coloured coat, its colour slightly brighter than his cap with the gleaming visor, "freshly polished," the inspector noted as the two men swung Momo onto the stretcher. He would have preferred not to hear the moan, but he told them, too late and stammering: "His shoulder... I forgot to tell you." They had already lifted the stretcher after buckling the three straps that protected the wounded man from falling or from any temptation to escape. Momo's groans had changed to a long scream of terror, unbearable in the calm bright morning. The inspector examined the rifle which was not much longer, end to end, than an old-fashioned Colt. He took out his cigar, spat in the snow, then, looking at the house, wide open now to anyone who might come by and being completely torn to pieces by the winter wind, he went back towards the house, forcing himself to place his feet in the deep prints left by Fred and Florent, "bears' paws," he thought, comparing them to the prints left by Marie-Rose, who had left the house without even closing the door. He sniffed at the empty flask, smiled briefly, put his foot on a slippery object and picked it up – a silver lighter with initials in stippled engraving: "M.R." on one side and "P" on the other, nothing more – then he noticed the parka on the armchair. The wind was blowing through the broken window and the door. "They spent the

113

night in here: he had his gun but she didn't have anything...her skin," he said, confused, suddenly blushing.

Sitting at the wheel of the car, eyes closed, he dreamed of
the day when he would be able to spend most of his time in
a little house nestled in a clump of trees, always green, waiting for his pension cheque, sitting in a comfortable chair,
with nothing to do between two photography sessions but
stir up the fire in the fireplace. "Other people's business,
I'm fed up with all that. And I don't intend to get mixed up
in this one. Just another six months, by God. On Saint-Jean
Baptiste Day. And I know one person that's going to be cel-
ebrating!" Lifting his hat he looked in the rear-view mirror
at his country notary's face, the blue eyes that seemed buried under heavy brow-ridges accentuated by thick eyebrows
that pointed towards the edges of his face like his
moustache, and the dimple in the middle of his chin.

5

Phonse sniffed the coffee steaming in the battered aluminum pot and pulled the suspenders of his black pants over his pinkish flannelette undershirt. They looked at one another. Phonse sat down at the table, cut himself a good-sized chunk of salt pork, which slopped onto his plate, then tore off a hunk of bread. "So," the inspector said, "it's today." Phonse shook his head, cheeks swollen by a mouthful of bread and pork, and said, "Tomorrow morning," adding as soon as he had swallowed, "It'd be a good thing if some people didn't show their face around here because even if I'm seventy years old..."

"Well, the way things are right now, I don't think that guy's gonna be getting into too much trouble."

Phonse coughed, then asked, rather annoyed: "So you finally nabbed him, after he done his dirty work, that goddamn savage!" The inspector drew up a chair and sat down, legs apart, casting a sidelong glance at the percolator. "A hot coffee'd taste good." Phonse rushed over to the stove, picked up the percolator and put it on the arborite table that had replaced the old maple one he'd sold to an auctioneer for a song, then took a cup down from the cupboard and filled it with thick brown steaming coffee. "After you've warmed up a little, if you aren't too tired, maybe I'll finally get to find out exactly what happened," Phonse said, hands on his knees.

"It's funny, Phonse, I was thinking you'd have a few things to tell me. Maybe I was wrong."

Phonse's hands moved along his thighs. He looked at the dead cigar that dangled from the corner of the inspector's mouth as he touched his burning cup. "What kind of gun do you use for hunting?" Once that was out he brought the cup to his lips and blew gently on the coffee. "What the hell's going on here? You got a nerve, asking the dead girl's father a thing like that. You out of your head?" He sighed as he reached for the fresh bread, the soft inside crumbling at his touch. "It's true, I said I was gonna get him. That I can't deny. But not till I bury my daughter. Don't worry, I know where that bastard's hanging out!" The inspector was uneasy, barely smiling; without realizing it he was ashamed of being so hard on Phonse, who'd had heart trouble for twenty years so people had got in the habit of treating him gently. "I have to do it, Phonse. Maurice was shot in the shoulder, just when I got there...And I'd heard you had some plans, so I came to see you...Specially because we haven't seen each other for a while. Must be two years now."

"Is he dead?"

"Sounds as if you'd like to finish him off."

Phonse burst out laughing, scratched his chest where the tuft of hair seemed to be itching. "That ain't gonna bring back my daughter, is it now? But if you wanta know, I really wouldn't care if that snot..."

"We won't get very far if we say so much the better, because you know, even if Momo killed Gigi..."

"What're you talkin' about – *if* Momo killed Gigi? Sounds like the police are protecting the thugs instead of us decent folks!"

He jumped to his feet, hand raised, as though he were about to attack the photograph of his daughter on the wall above the low cupboard. His leather boots creaked. "No if's about it. He done it. Who do *you* think it was? I'll swear on the Bible it was Momo."

116

"Come on, Phonse, even if you didn't want him to marry your daughter that's no reason to accuse him without any evidence."

Phonse sank back into his chair, his big stiff bony hands on his knees. "If you're lookin' for evidence I can give you all you want. First of all: anybody can tell you, Gigi didn't even want to hear his name when she found out about that robbery..."

"You sure about that?"

"Sure I'm sure! Gigi seen him once or twice so he wouldn't suspect nothing, you get it?"

"No, not really," the inspector replied.

The inspector's smile was worse than an insult – it was a way to discredit him, reduce everything he'd said to childish nonsense; then Phonse said, "Talkin' don't lead nowhere." "No, come on, now," the inspector insisted, all attention now, but not wanting to show too much meddling curiosity. "Go on, Phonse." He began: "Well, he knew you arrested him and the storekeeper recognized him cause Gigi'd talked. How'd I know that, eh? Well, she had to talk, don't you think? So there's one bit of evidence. You want some more? I never seen nobody as jealous as Momo, everybody knows that. Ask anybody. So that means when he gets out of jail, do you think he's satisfied to just call her up for a chat? He knows she's gone off to the city with some guy. A guy all dressed up like a big shot. Italian, I think. But that...takes all kinds to make a world. So, like I'm sayin', soon as he gets out of jail there he is, takes me by surprise. Don't look none too happy. He warns me if I don't tell him where she is there'll be trouble. So put yourself in my shoes: you do some fast thinkin'. I give him her address but I don't worry about it too much. I figure her Italian can look after her. I couldn't get in touch with her because she didn't give me her phone number. I could'a told her that wild Indian was goin' straight for her place. If I'd a known what store her Italian'd put her in..." He stopped when he heard the inspector sigh. "Go on, Phonse."

117

"Okay, where was I?"

"In the city."

"Hang on there, not so fast. He threatened to kill her if I didn't give him her address. 'I'll go and look her up myself but it won't be such a nice surprise for her,' he told me. If I'd'a been younger..."

"Then what?"

"You want me to skip some parts, eh?"

With his thumbs stuck under his suspenders, looking important, he went on: "We're coming to the proof, Paul-Emile. Drink up your coffee before it freezes. So, that nut's still on his way – keep that in your head, now – with her address wrote down on that letter she sent me. That clear enough for you?"

"It's interesting, anyway."

"It sure as hell is! With the address in his pocket, it ain't gonna take him too long to find her, right? And then he stabs her in the back. He's a maniac with a knife, that one. And the worst thing is, the city police, the whole force, when they phoned me up I already knew about it. Jos calls me, he says: 'You read the paper this mornin'?' I tell him: 'How'd you expect me to read the paper this mornin' or any other mornin'? You know I never had time to learn how to read. When I was ten years old I was already doin' a man's work.' He's a funny one, Jos. Takes his time: 'If you're standin' up I think you better sit down because I got somethin' to tell you and it's gonna be pretty hard to take.' So I say, 'Okay, go on, I can take it.' So he reads me what's in his paper. They didn't give her last name, just said she was called Gigi. Jos said maybe I wouldn't recognize her cause the picture just showed her back. When I got to the morgue there was no way out of it, I recognized her all right. Good thing her face wasn't touched. With a madman like that I was expectin' the worst. Florent brought her back yesterday."

His eyes were motionless, so liquid the inspector was afraid they would melt into the furrows of his hollow face beneath the flaccid, peeled-looking skin. "You knew Maurice had got there."

"Jos called me and told me everythin'. But you know, Paul-Emile, I get the feelin' you don't really care about Gigi bein' dead. Looks like you're more interested in catchin' the guy that shot Momo."

The inspector sighed, staring at the space between his wide-spread legs. "What happens in town, it's up to their police to take care of it. Everybody's got his own row to hoe. It's complicated enough already. Your gun's a twenty gauge, isn't it?"

"It's a twelve and you know it. You even sneaked a look at it when you come in."

"That the only one you got?"

"I was always satisfied with what I had."

The inspector took an unwrapped cigar out of his inside pocket, stuck it in the corner of his mouth and lit it, blinking at the pungent smoke. "Well, my friend, it isn't because I'm getting bored, but I gotta be on my way. I knew your daughter when she was a little girl, and it hurts, Phonse. An only child, eh?" But his question seemed to float between them, useless. The silence was dragging on when Phonse started, as though stung by a wasp in his half-sleep, and he took the inspector's hand. "Tomorrow morning at nine. You're comin', eh? Florent looked after everythin'. She looks almost alive. You don't want a bite before you go? It's no bother, Paul-Emile." The inspector removed his hand from Phonse's hesitant grasp and was sucking gently on the rather dry cigar which sputtered as it was consumed, nervously pushing back his hat and sticking it on his head as he walked backwards towards the door, as though he were running away from Phonse, seized by a sudden hunger: "I ain't sayin' this because it's my daughter, but she knew where she had to go if she wanted to get somethin' out of life, and me, old as I am, I told her she oughtta stay here. I was scared for her. When you're in the city it don't matter if you know what you want, sometimes you get a surprise, but

119

that didn't bother her none; she said in her letter, 'Don't get yourself in a sweat, Pa, I'm working so I can buy a duplex.' See, what she had in mind was to bring me to the city. Can you see that, Phonse spendin' the rest of his life in town? See, I didn't have the heart to tell her, but as far as I was concerned, her nice house, you know...Maybe she told me so I'd know she hadn't forgot about me, even if I couldn't give her very much except for her skin and bones. Her flesh, she got that from her mother. Bertha was the one that read me her letter; poor Bertha, she didn't know how to tell me the news that Jos'd already passed on." It was time for him to stop talking, the inspector thought, wringing his gloves, terrified at the tears glistening in the grey of Phonse's eyes, preferring a boot in the rear to consoling a man in his underwear, bigger than him, at least ten years older, whose skin had stayed white in spite of the years he'd spent in the open air, ploughing and splitting wood. Even his hands with their spots, their curved shape, their reddish hairs, hadn't turned brown – resistant to the sun, the wind and the cold, they were only hardened or encrusted. He raised his right hand and rubbed his eyes, so hard the inspector thought for a moment he was going to pull off the eyelid. "All right," he sighed, "I won't keep you any longer," and pulled his hat down over his forehead before he went out. The sparkling snow blinded him and he had to stop for a moment, his arm stretched out before him, thinking: "Still, it's not so complicated. Aren't that many 30.30's around here." Then he slowly started his car, turning in front of Phonse's house, and went back towards the barely awakened village, the houses seeming so snug in the midst of the snowbanks, with their smoking chimneys, all isolated and yet brought together in the same natural shelter at the foot of the mountains, as though out of range of the wind. "If Jérôme isn't up yet, well, I'll just smash the door down," he thought, a little embarrassed to be going to the Hôtel right away, when there were still other fish to fry – Marie-Rose, who had disappeared without saying goodbye, Calixa who hadn't shown his face, probably because Ti-Pit hadn't had the time or the chance to tell him about his younger brother's accident, and the owner of the 30.30 who might be sleeping peacefully while he waited. It had been a good while since he'd seen Emérence, her thick auburn chignon, her dress open to reveal an overflowing bosom, "a real loaf of bread, still hot, fresh from the oven," and he lingered, remembering the smooth skin of that dough which swelled with every breath, as though it had a life of its own. He sighed: "And to think, I was too dumb back in those days to stop Jérôme from putting the ring on her finger, too dumb to..." He stopped just in front of the Hôtel, leaving the car there so that Fred wouldn't waste two hours trying to find him when he came back from the hospital.

His fear was realized: no light in the main room of the Hôtel, the door still locked. "Well, kiddies, sorry to get you out of bed, but I need a good cup of coffee and Emérence, you're the only one that knows how to make it the way I like it." And he pressed the bell-button with his thumb for several seconds, telling himself that after all, it isn't every day an old friend comes for breakfast. First he saw big Jérôme, as broad as two months earlier, coming down the stairs at the back of the room, dressing-gown hanging loosely over his striped pyjamas, then he saw the face of Emérence in the kitchen doorway. Already up, she must have made the coffee, "at least we've got that," he thought as big Jérôme unlocked the door, looking grumpy, and he hid behind it, a broad smile making his face round now, "a real jack-o'lantern."

"Well, this is a surprise!" Jérôme exclaimed as soon as the inspector had raised his hat. "Emérence, come see what the wind blew in! It's Paul-Emile!"

The kitchen door remained closed. Not the slightest sound. Jérôme hurried as fast as he could with the belly that no belt could contain swaying from left to right like a pudding that hadn't set. He opened the door just enough to stick his head inside, and muttered something, then went back to the inspector who had taken off his hat and gloves in preparation for the appearance of Emérence. "Come on, take off your coat!" Jérôme purred. "Just a couple of minutes and my good wife'll bring you something to eat. You know how it is, she hasn't fixed herself or nothing, better she doesn't show her face yet. Women! You're lucky, Paul-Emile, you don't know what it's like!" The inspector smiled with the corner of his mouth, just where he was going to stick a half-smoked cigar when Jérôme shouted to him, clasping his hands as though he were clutching a ball: "Don't light that, I got a real beauty from Havana, Cuba." Then he disappeared behind the bar; the inspector heard him breathing noisily, as though each intake of breath were feeding a motor that couldn't start, "his lungs must be all clogged up, buried under all that fat," he thought as the hotelkeeper rifled through everything he touched without unearthing his box of cigars. Finally he got up, face glistening and red, looking annoyed; he pounded the arborite counter with his soft white fist and pushed open the kitchen door. The inspector could hear outbursts of muffled voices and he smiled, almost relieved to be present, even at a distance, at an exchange of views that was more conjugal than loving. When Jérôme came out he was different, silently obedient; gesturing to his guest to be patient, he climbed up the long staircase that led to the floor where for seven dollars excluding tip, you could, in the slow season, have a room and even a fairly generous breakfast – two eggs, bacon, cheese, jam, not to mention the big bowl of porridge, specialty of the landlady who judged a customer according to whether or not he asked for more. After gulping down two bowls of porridge and all the rest, the inspector always had the comforting impression that he had gained an hour, because he could go without dinner. And as there was some danger that the day was going to be a full one, he thought that Emérence's breakfast came at a good time. She walked in just then, having taken care to make herself presentable, wearing her emerald-green dressing gown, closed at the waist but wide open over the nightgown she had apparently neglected to button. "Still in good shape, Emérence," the inspector said, smiling as though he had got up early just to be able to come out with this polite expression which had become a kind of password between them. And her reply was invariably the same, in the same sprightly tone: "Oh, we get by, even if it isn't New Year's Day every morning."

"All the better," he said, pulling out a chair for her and bending over her shoulder as far as his modesty would permit. As soon as she was sitting down, with an instinctive gesture, as though to correct the indiscretion he had committed, she raised her long hand to the visible part of her bosom, frowning, annoyed, almost sullen, and said in a strangely capricious voice: "You aren't spoiling us these days. When was the last time you came to see us?" Flattered at her impatience he nodded: "A month, maybe a bit longer."

"A month! You sure don't spend your life down here. The last time you showed your face, must have been back in the middle of November."

"Could be."

And suddenly, remembering a serious oversight, she pushed back her chair: "Dear Lord! Where's my head this morning? I don't suppose you've even had breakfast yet."

"If it isn't too much trouble..."

"Trouble! You sound like a total stranger. I suppose you're here because of Maurice?"

He merely nodded as she walked away, erect and proud, her chignon held in place by the tortoise-shell clip he had brought her two years earlier when he came to arrest Momo and which she had worn ever since, at least whenever he stopped at the Hôtel du Nord. "I was dumb then!" he thought as Jérôme came back downstairs, holding a box of cigars against his chest.

6

The inspector's arrival opened the circle of smokers. He breathed in the dry smell of *canadien* tobacco – "naturally strong " – consenting reluctantly to join the men who had been arguing there for some time, all wearing identical black suits, a little shiny at the elbows, and white shirts with collars starched so stiff that the narrow neckties seemed to hang limply from them. "So," Ti-Pit began, unrecognizable in his mourning clothes, "still no news? But if you wanta know what we think, Inspector, the guy that shot Momo ain't from around here. We think it's that gang from Montreal. Whaddaya say about that?" The inspector had taken off his grey tweed coat, hesitating so they would think he was considering what Ti-Pit had just said on their behalf.

"Hard to say," he concluded, walking over to hang his coat on the already overloaded rack.

He was silent when Phonse walked out of the funeral parlour, more bent than ever, long arms dangling, and came into the smoking-room, not seeming to understand what was going on or where he was. Simply dazed, depressed by the evidence of death, by Gigi's stillness although Florent and his sons had managed if not to revive her, at least to make her as *natural* as she'd been in life. Jérôme broke the circle and walked forward with his surging gait, the result of an effort of his entire being, towards Phonse, who stood

124

there staring above the inspector's Tyrolean hat at something that must have been the reference point for his daydreams. "Poor Phonse," Jérôme said, "here, come and sit with us."

Phonse followed him dutifully, let himself be dragged rather by the hotelkeeper, who put his arm around Phonse's and led him to the other end of the smoking-room where the old men were drawing energetically on their pipes to prove to themselves that they still had some breath to spare, that it wasn't time yet to keep vigil over their earthly remains. Silently the inspector crossed the few feet separating him from the parlour, took his hands out of his pockets before entering the room, head bent as though he were afraid of bumping into something, gripped by the dense, sickening aroma of the bunches of flowers hung on the wall with black taffeta above the coffin that was open as far as the dead girl's waist. He spent a few minutes looking, feeling nothing: her face was a little swollen, rouged, lips closed, the upper one slightly thicker than the other, like her father's; then he saw Jérôme drifting towards him, eyes piously lowered as though he had been overcome, the inspector thought, by a pity that suited him about as well as a bikini. "You can go if you want; I'll stay and watch," he whispered with an air of suffering and complicity. The inspector patted his jacket pocket, touched his forehead in a kind of awkward salutation to the dead woman, then tiptoed out of the room, picking up his hat and coat on the way, putting them on when he was on the gallery safe from other people's eyes. "Guess I'll go and see how my Emérence is getting along all by herself," he thought.

Jérôme hadn't raised his eyes, even after the inspector's departure, expecting to see Gigi open hers, stare at him as her father had stared at the wall earlier. "Is it my fault if that madman had to go and look her up so he could play games with his knife?" he pleaded within himself, not certain, however, that his own hands were clean, remembering that Emérence had kicked her out because of him, pushing

her right into the arms of the polite Italian dressed like a
fashion-plate with whom she had disappeared in that bot-
tle-green Triumph. "A man's a man, you can't do nothin'
about that, and anyway she was the kind of a girl that can't
help making men behave a certain way," he thought as he
unbuttoned the collar of his shirt, which was so tight it was
choking him. It had been a bad fall. Hardly any hunters.
Not a soul in the hotel after ten o'clock. Rain two days out
of three. And no question of warming yourself up in bed
with the landlady. Peace and quiet they certainly had,
more than enough. "That's when I got my bright idea,"
and he smiled, eyes closed, as though he were illuminated
from within by a beatific vision – a parade of girls in bath-
ing suits on the biggest table in the grill, girls from Saint-
Emmanuel and the surroundings exhibiting their pale
flesh, swaying on their high heels, trying to smile at the
exclusively male gathering – male with the exception of the
boss's wife grumbling behind the bar. These men had nothing better to do than drink and drink as they argued the
respective merits of the contestants among whom, it was
generally considered, at least according to Jérôme who led
the discussion, "Gigi stood out like a rose in the desert," and
she had finally been crowned Queen of the North, a title
awarded for the first time in the county. But that wasn't all:
in spite of the racket he had made a speech to announce
that in addition to her title, the queen would have the privilege of serving customers at the Hôtel du Nord. The other
girls were lifted off the table by several chivalrous men
anxious to console them, telling them their turn would
come next year. Gigi stood alone, hands on her hips, looking above them, smiling, or so it seemed, at an old dream
that was finally within her reach. Jérôme had to climb
laboriously onto the table to kiss her and ask if she
accepted. She said simply yes. There was no question of
wages. Emérence, reluctant at first to go along with his
idea, had finally got used to seeing a strange woman wandering through the Hôtel, serving men at the bar and at the

126

tables, and she had even taken advantage of the opportunity to unload on Gigi the burden of cleaning the rooms. It could have gone on like that, but early in the summer he had thought it would be good business to rent one of his lots to a person named Boudrias; that morning as he was shaving in the room where he slept alone because Emérence was afraid of being smothered under his weight, old Manchotte had driven up in his buggy like a bat out of hell, tied the reins to a post on the gallery and run in. He thought when he noticed him: "I should'a known...The old man's pissed off because he's got a neighbour across the way, and now he's come to raise hell. I should'a given him that lot, eh? We should'a told him to get lost when he came here but we're nice people, too nice. And one of these days we're gonna pay for it." And he stayed in his room, hands moist, puffing on his cigar and sweating in his dressing-gown. Then Manchotte went back down the stairs, a small dried-up man, childish looking despite his sixty-five years, his face almost black in the shadow of the felt hat pulled down over his eyes. Jérôme got a good look at him, hidden behind the purple flowered curtains; in particular he could see the brown stream he let fall on the stairs. Manchotte bit at his plug of tobacco, then stuck it in the back pocket of his overalls, and as he paced back and forth between his dark brown mare with its yellowish, vomit-coloured spots and the staircase, he chewed on his tobacco, swinging the stump of his amputated arm with the iron hook attached, then stopped to spit deliberately onto the gallery, as though he anticipated cornering Jérôme in a duel this way. Jérôme saw himself walking down the stairs, chest thrust out, shouting to Manchotte to clear out before something bad happened, but he couldn't move, imprisoned as he was in his fear, behind the curtains, thinking: "The rotten bastard, that rotten old bastard...Go ahead and spit! But you'll be sorry one of these days, I promise you," and wiped his hands on his pyjamas. Manchotte was still chewing, walking, pacing. Jérôme slumped onto his bed, his widower's

127

bed as he called it, forehead and neck dripping with sweat, convinced it was the damp July heat more than his fear that was causing his discomfort. He decided to stay inside till Manchotte left. "The old lady can look after things by herself for once. Everybody gets his turn..." But as he waited he wondered what he could do – lie on his back, arms crossed behind his head and smoke – the life of a pasha – and they'd bring him his meals on a tray, if you please. "After all, who's the boss?" Someone knocked at the door and he held his breath, fists clenched on his chest, terrified by the sound of his pounding heart, louder than the clock, and feeling tense, stiff, as though his mass of fat had melted or changed into a shuddering bundle of nerves. Another knock, barely audible, brought him to this feet, furious at the contempt he felt for himself, realizing abruptly that Manchotte wouldn't have hesitated for a moment if he'd really wanted to come in. He opened the door with an enormous sigh: "Ah, it's just you, Gigi." She looked at him, then said, "You're as white as a sheet." He chewed on his dead cigar as he rubbed his chest. "I don't feel right this morning. My heart's pounding, you can't imagine what it's like. Shut the door." She did so, waiting for him to feel a little better before saying: "Your wife told me to tell you there's a man wants to talk to you, and she said maybe it'd be a good idea to take care of it right away." He didn't react, hands still holding back the pulsations of his heart, while she looked in spite of herself at the enormous belly swelling his pyjamas. He dropped his hands and said, red with anger: "What's going on in that woman's head, will you tell me? If I stay in bed I got a reason, haven't I? But try and tell her anything! Touch my forehead. My temperature must be a hundred and two, a hundred and three. Come on, don't be scared, touch it!" And taking her hand he forced her to touch his greasy forehead. "I'm burning up, can't you feel it?"

"A little," she admitted, removing her hand.

"What'd I tell you? You go tell her I'm stayin' in bed

today. Hold on...bring up a bottle of Black and White. Don't forget, and get a move on, honey."

He sent her away with a pat on the behind but afterwards, when the door was closed and locked, his hands were itching. "What kept me back, will you tell me? When I think about that woman, lets me do it one a month, doesn't move a finger, just lays there like she was dead. Like it was some kind'a chore. That's laziness, it's sick!" And he burst out laughing. "Yes, it's sick!" He promised to tell her that next time and just as he was about to slump onto the bed again, a knock at the door made him start. Breathless, her cheeks as red as her short wavy hair – it was long now, and so curly it formed a wreath around her face – Gigi held out a glass of water and two aspirins, tiny white buttons in the fleshy folds of her hand. "Ah, that old woman!" he said, trembling with rage. "We'll see who wears the pants around here! Go get me that bottle I asked you for. Tell her she'll hear from me when I'm back on my feet." He was on his feet, however, gesticulating, wearing his satin bathrobe. "You want me to tell her just like that?" Gigi asked in an incredulous tone that was nearly sorrowful, although it didn't prevent him from insisting: "All you gotta do is tell her what I just told you. No problem." She was putting the glass of water and the aspirins on the dresser when he asked her, mollified: "You scared of her, eh?" She shook her head – neither yes nor no. "You like it here, working at the Hôtel, though?" And before she even risked an answer, he added: "You couldn't find nothin' better for twenty miles. Even if you ain't earnin' as much money as an MP..." With a wave of his hands he took the words out of her mouth, saying: "You're gonna tell me you work long hours. That's true. I got eyes, I can see. In fact, I was just thinkin' about that when you went downstairs – who's the boss, eh? – I was tellin' myself you deserved a good five bucks more a week. But don't think that's a present I'm givin' you!" He put out his cigar in the bluish glass ashtray, his face turned towards her, trying to smile at him as she moved away from

129

his advancing hand. She seemed ashamed, but he could feel that he had already won her, that she was not so much frightened as frozen in the weakness of her servant's position. He moved his hand, breathing his own sweat mixed with the smell of cold cigar, and he guessed by the way she was staring at him that she was ready to do anything, except resist. A broad smile split his pumpkin face, as Emérence called him when she wanted to put him in his place. "You look scared. A big girl like you, ain't you ashamed of yourself? I bet you don't run away like that when Momo..." His belly was pressing her against the door; she was soft and warm, and he told her, his mouth close to her forehead: "Did you know you got a good build for a girl these days?" She looked down, her mouth partly opened, not resisting the pressure he was exerting to spread her legs. And as he pressed her shoulders against the door he whispered in her ear: "Come on, honey, go ahead." Then he was silent, his breath coming too hard, not even answering her: "You think so?" but thinking nevertheless: "Of course I do, I don't think about nothin' else." And he burst out in a laugh that came from his belly, enormous and surging. She put a warm hand on his arm.

Jérôme opened his eyes, untied the narrow knot of his black tie and looked down, noting that she was sleeping the same deep sleep, her mouth sewn shut, hands crossed, entwined in the long rosary with its fine vermeil beads. The light was sparkling on the silver cross. He closed his eyes again, kneeling now at the prie-Dieu, his head in his hands; though prostrate with humiliation he thought, "Good God, is it my fault if my wife rationed me and I let myself be tempted by a new body?" and the shame he felt was nothing after he had evoked the "new body"; his memory slipped back to the red hair where he had buried his face, unable to control his breathing, while his hand popped the buttons on her blouse like corks and rubbed the round breast, with no protruberance, just softer, smoother flesh, so smooth he had begun to think the nipple hadn't sprouted yet, and then he felt the granular bud sticking to his damp palm. He took her hand and guided it underneath his belly, into the opening in his pyjamas where, heavy and erect, the muscle of his sex enlarged and grew as she pressed it with mechanical regularity. Then he whimpered: "Go on, you fuckin' pig!" He pounded his head against the walnut door, and she went on blindly emptying him of the very substance of his desire, though he repeated to her: "You going crazy?" He moved back, his face hot, and then looking at her, unwrapped a cigar and thanked her in his fashion: "You're pretty good at it. Now go downstairs, hurry up, and bring me that bottle." She tucked her blouse back inside her creased skirt, saying peevishly: "I can't let your wife see me like this with my tits hanging out."

"Go and change then, but hurry up!"

And without bothering to bolt the door, getting his breath back a little at a time, he opened the curtains just enough to see Manchotte looking towards the bedroom window from under the brim of his grey hat, "like he smells something fishy," Jérôme thought, hiding behind the curtains again, the sun barely filtering through them, lighting them like a stained-glass window. He remembered, almost two years later, how he had kicked the empty space, then collapsed into a thickly padded chair, bought at an auction for three times what it was worth because of the claim that it dated back to Confederation and there, the cigar still unlighted in his mouth, he began to regret not taking better advantage of the situation five minutes earlier, thinking: "We'll take a rain check, honey." He laughed his coarse laugh then, choking, from the belly, and gratified to hear himself in such a good mood, he prolonged his pleasure by remembering Gigi's nose, turned up and pointed, "her only flaw." He kept laughing for another moment, imagining himself with her right under his wife's nose, something that did happen a month later when they found themselves in the same posture, this time leaning against the refrigerator, both of them sure that Emérence had gone to the store, to

Joseph's. "But by God it wasn't funny that time. The wife really got on her high horse. 'Aren't you ashamed, you pigs, carrying on like that behind my back? But your dirty little games are over now, because you, you little bitch, you're going out that door before I slit your throat!' Gigi didn't hang around to be told twice. That was when her Spaghetti took her off to the city, poor little girl, all the same... Wasn't her fault if her mother died young, and Phonse always had his hands all over her. He's the one that made her like that. After all, nobody was forcing her to do it. It didn't bother her, specially because her Momo was far away, she needed it likely," and he opened his eyes again, catching a glimpse between his spread fingers of the turned up, pointed nose; then he was suddenly seized by a hysterical fit of laughter, despite the presence of Louis-Joseph who was standing on his left, examining Gigi without paying him the slightest attention. "Just as wild as his nephews," Jérôme was thinking, "people that think they're I don't know what, better'n the rest of us, the way they brag." But old Bautront didn't move, his thumb stuck in the black, worn-down bowl of the pipe he had kept in the hollow of his hand even on his last two wedding days; it symbolized his indifference to the opinion of the entire village, his insistence on remaining as alone as when he was born in the shadow of a Detroit spinning mill, so deliberately alone that he preferred to leave Saint-Emmanuel rather than depend on the village which, by way of revenge, had named him The Beggar – although even when he was reduced to penury he would tolerate neither assistance nor the slightest allusion to his fate. No one, not even his own family, had ever known where he would be the next day or what boss would be hare-brained enough to take him on only to hear, a week or a month later, that he'd had it up to here with picking tobacco or haying. The only work he had done consistently, with visible pleasure, was what he did for himself, all alone, with no one to tell him how to do it: working in the bush, stripping off the branches, sawing, siding and carting away the trees that died every year in the huge bush that belonged to his boy Freddie; he would spend the fall days splitting and cording in preparation for the long months of cold, going to the village only to buy his tobacco, salt pork and potatoes, or something to drink from his nephew Calixa, son of his sister-in-law and cousin who had disappeared so long ago he barely remembered her.

And while Jérôme was inwardly slandering the entire Bautront family and all their relations, furious at being on his knees behind Louis-Joseph, as though he were humiliated in his presence, Bertha came in, escorted by all the able-bodied men who were tired of smoking and chatting. Accidentally or not, she struck Louis-Joseph with her elbow and he turned around to face them all, not addressing anyone in particular: "It had to happen." Not another word. Just an allusion, but all the more scandalous because no one wanted to suspect that Momo might be innocent. In the total silence their breathing was audible. Joseph, known as Chaise-longue, nodded his head like a good businessman while Bertha seemed to be expecting something else of him, but no one dared make any reply, as though only Louis-Joseph Bautront could allow himself to differ so arrogantly from all the rest of the village – and do it out loud, in the presence of the dead woman's father who had prudently taken refuge in his mute insistent sorrow. Jérôme turned his head as Louis-Joseph looked his way before leaving the room, walking lightly and silently. Jérôme saw him empty his pipe into the standing ashtray, fill it but not light it, and leave the place, shoving his hat right down to his ears. Then Jérôme, who had got to his feet, shook his head, saying clearly enough to be understood: "At his age he oughtta be more respectful," but aside from Bertha who merely sighed, no one seemed to grasp the meaning of his remark. "You can tell Jérôme don't come from around here," Chaise-longue thought, tired already from spending more than five minutes on his feet without opening his mouth.

The afternoon was darkened by large white clouds

caught between the mountains. Joseph pushed open the door of the store, complaining, "We're in for a big one." But the inspector just raised his hat rapidly and kept searching through the pile of checked wool shirts. Then he let out a long sigh, as though he had just missed finding what he wanted. "You need some clothes for the winter?" Joseph asked, his coat off now, his shoulders slumping under the white silk scarf with its greyish fringes.

"I was just having a look at what you got."

"That's all right, go on."

Joseph walked around the display of bolts of fabric to the stoneware pot where he filled his only pipe, its bowl as large as an apple; it held two or three normal portions of tobacco, so that he didn't have to get up once he was in his rocking chair. He had enough for a good couple of hours of peaceful smoking, sometimes even longer, especially when a customer or an ordinary visitor made him forget to light his pipe. He sat down, head bent, drew out the flame of his lighter, gazing at the inspector who was now leaning against one of the pillars that held up the shelves piled with all kinds of clothing – drill pants, overalls, sweaters gaudily decorated with animals, grey-and-white wool socks, boots and rubbers. "You and Marie-Rose been engaged for a long time now?" the inspector asked. Phil didn't take his eyes off the knife he had been sharpening since the inspector's arrival; Joseph grasped the arms of his chair, his chest out, talking with his pipe still in his mouth: "Don't talk to me about that little chippy or I'll start using bad words!"

"Sorry, but I have to talk about her."

"I figure it's been three months at least," Phil said at last, not looking up.

"And when's the wedding?"

Joseph struck the arm of his chair with his elbow and leaped to his feet, his self-esteem wounded to the core: "There ain't gonna be no weddin', you got that through your skull? It's finished! I'd rather have my son a bachelor for the rest of his life than a laughin'-stock." Phil dropped

134

the long carving knife onto the hollowed, scratched wood of the chopping block and stared at his father: "It so happens that I ain't changed my plans." Joseph was shaking, spilling ashes onto his hand. "That's right, kill your old father who's given you everythin'!"

"Come on, M'sieu Lavallée, let him talk."

"Let him talk, the bugger! Just let him try and show me his fiancée isn't the worst tramp we've seen around here since Gigi."

Phil looked at the knife he was holding, hands stretched out flat on the chopping block. "Marie-Rose's too good. She went and took him something to eat and I guess when she got there she got scared."

"Scared of what?" the inspector asked.

"Scared of me. Since we were supposed to be spendin' the rest of the evening together."

"What did you think when you saw she was late?"

"Well, I didn't really know what was goin' on. I phoned the Café Central and Ti-Paul told me she'd left in a hurry."

The inspector encouraged him to go on, but Joseph was pointing the curved stem of his pipe, which filled his entire hand, at his son. "And he was awake the whole blessed night on account of that little chippy that's gonna turn out just like Gigi; I heard him walkin' back and forth..."

"All night long?"

"Just about. Quite a while, anyways. One time I even thought I heard him goin' out. But I must'a made a mistake. He's too chicken-hearted to do that."

And turning towards the inspector who had paid so little attention to him, listening almost absent-mindedly, he cleared his throat: "Now you listen here, we don't have to tell you everything that goes on here. Why do you want to know all that anyways?" The inspector seemed to hesitate for a moment then, looking down at his dead cigar: "I was a little worried about Marie-Rose. She looked scared when I saw her. Likely thought Phil was gonna call off the engagement, I couldn't really figure it out." Joseph sat down again, grumbling: "She can just stay out of it, that one; it was shameful what she did. If Phil ain't got enough self-respect to tell her to go to hell, well I ain't got another word to say." The pungent smell of meat made the inspector feel sick, and he lit his cigar, unable to take his eyes off the thick, red chunks which seemed almost alive under Phil's big hands. His reddened fingernails were sunk deep in it. Phil tested the blade of the knife against his thumb, then cut a quarter of beef, which fell into the pool of blood with a splash. "If ever," said Joseph, sunk back in his chair, a blanket over his knees as though he were a dried-up old woman, "if you ever nab the guy that shot Momo, you can thank him for me. Good riddance. He ain't like The Breeze. Him, at least, you hardly ever see." Feeling vaguely sick, the inspector pushed the brim of his hat back on his broad forehead and opened the door. "You don't want a wool shirt for the winter?"

"Next time," he said, closing the door, relieved to be breathing fresh air, but disappointed too at not having pushed Phil to the wall; but how? "He didn't seem like a guy that's made up his mind to marry a virgin...But he still messes around in the meat with his fingernails full of blood."

Florent's ambulance was parked in front of the funeral home. "Fred must be in there spying. I've got half a mind to let him make a fool of himself," and he walked past the only brick house in the village without stopping, walking rapidly, an unusual sight in the seemingly sleeping village on this dark afternoon with snow in the air; but as soon as he was ensconced in the warmth of the Café Central he relaxed, sitting in a corner, waiting for Marie-Rose to appear. "She looks tired." There were shadows under her eyes: her pale, waxy skin accentuated her hollow cheeks. Her order pad helped her put on a bold front. "I can't think about nothing else, I can still see him with his eyes open, not even able to talk...Who could'a done it, you got any idea?" He touched her hand, but she recoiled, as though

136

any contact were repugnant or a fatal reminder of Momo's grimacing face, his staring, bulging eyes. "Sit down a minute," he told her. She turned – a long circular glance that recorded the total emptiness of the room – then sat down across from him, elbows on the table, perched on the edge of the red moleskin seat, black along the seams, and he noticed her arched foot, ready to lift her out of her seat if a customer came in, or Paul who was always watching to be sure she wasn't wasting time; even when there wasn't a soul in the restaurant he always found something for her to do, even if it was only washing the clean ashtrays or tidying up the counter by the cash register.

"What're you eating?"

As though she didn't suspect that he had invited her to sit down so he could ask her for something besides an ordinary bowl of soup or the indigestible home-made pizza that Paul had thought it necessary to include on the menu after the Hôtel Mamma Potenza began to attract all the village young people and visitors on summer evenings; it offered Johnny Grisarelli's orchestra as well as pizza that was kneaded before their very eyes in the little pizzeria adjoining the dance hall. "Listen," said the inspector, "if you want to do something for Momo, it's easy; you just gotta make Phil talk."

"I don't even want to hear Phil's name again. I had enough of him."

She stared at him, her pointed chin resting in the palm of her hand, her black curls trembling at her slightest movement, like angel's hair, he thought, on the branches of a Christmas tree. "How do you expect Phil to help you? He could never stand Momo, and after what's happened, your timing's pretty bad."

"You don't have to ask him right out. If you see him, though, just try and see how he takes it when you tell him Momo was a real man. We'll see what happens."

She shook her head. "I can tell you right now what he's gonna say: if Momo was so smart how come you didn't

137

marry him. Or something like that."

"Doesn't hurt to try," the inspector answered, doing nothing to keep her there, not even raising a hand to help relieve her of the tremendous fatigue weighing on her shoulders, too embarrassed at her tear-filled eyes. "Just a dish of pea soup," he said gently. "Here," and he gave her the silver lighter, still warm from the pocket of his trousers.

7

"And I rushed through my lunch," he thought as he noticed Fred sitting at the bar, "still talking about his exploits while nobody can contradict him." Emérence was on the other side of the counter listening to him, her long hands crossed in front of her as though she were holding a microphone; she stopped looking at Fred as soon as the inspector came over, his hand on his hat by way of greeting. Fred, bare-headed, a ridge in his hair where the cap had squeezed his skull, straightened up in a military way, without, however, getting to his feet; he waited, rather pale, and saw the beginning of a smile that grew broader, creasing the inspector's cheek; he had to tolerate the inspector's irony, the almost vulgar way he had of putting him down publicly. "So, Fred, what's new?" "How about you? Find out anything?" He said it in one burst, in a threatening tone that astonished him so much that he nervously stuck the tip of his tongue onto the end of his narrow moustache, then chewed on it. "Me?" the inspector asked, his neck sticking out of the creamy dark brown woollen scarf folded loosely over his chest. "Me?" and he moved his hand, opening it under Fred's nose. "Can't you guess? A 30.30 cartridge. Still warm when I found it; you know where?" Emérence leaned over his arm to examine the cartridge in the hollow of his hand. "It isn't hot but it isn't cold either. On the ground, in front of the window in that little shack

139

behind the spruce trees." Fred replaced his cap, the damp tip of his moustache turning cold against his skin.

"Well, well!"

"Yeah," the inspector sighed. "But it doesn't tell me who was holding the gun. Or if Momo's recovered."

Fred remained pensive, sitting very straight on his stool, as though he had to decide whether he could satisfy the curiosity of his superior who was saying, unsmiling: "That's it for today?" Fred raised his head: "The doctor says the shoulder-blade's broken. A fracture, but not too serious." Then in an obvious effort at good will, he added: "I don't think it's those guys from the city, because if they'd'a wanted to they would have wiped him out before, don't you think?" The inspector shrugged, impatient: "We aren't here to think, Fred, we're here to pick up people that go around acting crazy, you understand?" Emérence had moved away from the counter, ill at ease, feeling she was in the way. "A brandy, Emérence, if it isn't too much trouble." She turned around to choose his favourite brand. Fred was leaning on the counter, considering his own reflection in the mirror, looking like a boy too serious for his age, he thought, in spite of the fine moustache that looked from a distance like a swelling, as though the upper lip were protruding. The inspector had moved and was sitting now on the furthest stool from Fred's, at the other end of the counter, absorbed in an apparently urgent and intimate conversation with Emérence, who was sitting across from him, face to face, forgetting Fred there as though he were just another customer passing through or one of the card-players at the back of the room who broke the silence abruptly from time to time by slapping down their cards without warning.

Fred didn't dare look at himself in the mirror any longer; eyes lowered, staring at his cap, he told himself he'd come back to the village prepared to do anything that would shed some light on that business which seemed to have lost all importance for the inspector. He had been ready to do anything after he'd seen Momo grimacing with pain on the stretcher they'd used to transport him, almost carelessly, to the emergency room where no one knew what to do with a wounded man, at least until Fred spoke rather abruptly to the intern who was strutting about, joking with the nurses in the office of the so-called reception area. And after he'd made sure they'd look after the wounded man, he had to buy two coffees for Florent to keep him another few minutes as they waited for news from the doctor, a tall Black who had wiped his gold-rimmed glasses before saying: "Don't worry about him. A simple fracture of the shoulder-blade." He hadn't dared go to visit him; Florent was getting impatient, one foot already out the door. And he had come back, sitting next to Florent this time, neither of them saying a word, retracing their route, less relieved than he had imagined at no longer having to tolerate the sight of Momo imprisoned in the straps of the stretcher, gasping every time the ambulance hit a bump on the gravel road, which was so slippery in places that he thought: "That's it, we're heading for the ditch." But Florent always straightened out the car and Fred would wait fearfully for the next swerve, sitting very erect on the wooden bench parallel to the stretcher, his feet on the floor, leg muscles tense, looking out the rear window at the road that wound through the snow like an endless ribbon of greyish brown with foam along the edges. He could hear Momo's laboured breathing under the blanket. And suddenly, in a turn so abrupt that the ambulance reared up, on the point of rolling over on its side, Fred was thrown forward against the stretcher. Momo screamed, then moaned, a hiccup expressing his pain. Fred sat up, legs wobbly, and pounded the window separating him from Florent who was either indifferent to the uproar of their speed or deafened by it, the back of his neck straight and white where the hair was freshly cut. He barely slowed down when they crossed the raised wooden bridge, although Fred pounded even harder with his fist at the risk of breaking the thick glass that cut him off and made him feel totally, exasperatingly impotent. Then the glass dropped down slowly, soundlessly, as though Florent had nothing to do with it. He leaned on his arm, as though to help it disappear and keep it there where it had disappeared. "Not so fast! The poor guy's suffering, it's pitiful," he shouted, and this was confirmed by Momo's gasping, fretful breathing; but the tires continued to send the gravel flying over the winding road. Fred clutched the edge of the bench and waited for Florent to slow down or stop devouring the road with his eyes. "He had to make that noise to drown out Momo," he realized now, forgetting, or making himself believe that he had been able to put up with Momo's constant hoarse complaints. And then it was as if the ambulance flowed onto a smooth, almost padded surface where the gravel road ran into the asphalt, and he relaxed. The noise was gone, that deafening, incessant metallic shudder. A gentle stretch between trees – spruce trees which reminded him, as they moved away from them, of a kind of fur growing over the countryside to protect it. Momo tried to say something, his mouth gaping open, but so softly that Fred had to bend over him and stick his ear close to Momo's brown face, with its sharp features under the fine layer of flesh stretched over the bones. He thought he heard, "I'm choking, I'm choking," and looking at Florent staring steadily at the road, he unfastened the straps, particularly the one that was squeezing Momo's chest. "Is that better?" he asked, with a guilty smile that was reflected again now in the large mirror lit by a string of round coloured lights. He had added: "They'll fix you up, it won't be long. We're just about there." He wished Florent would put up the window again. Momo had managed to free his left hand and it was searching under the blanket for the wound. Fred stroked Momo's shoulder with his fingertips, for fear of burning himself; and since he was unable to bring him any relief, even temporary, he repeated, "There, there..." looking grieved, as though these few words were enough to lessen the pain or at least make it more bearable.

But at the same time he was annoyed at himself for feeling unable to complete the mission the inspector had given him. "If he thinks this is the time to make somebody talk..." He knew practically nothing of the whole business, just that they were supposed to arrest Maurice Boulanger. And when Momo began to speak in his soft voice, interrupted by moans, he simply listened, nodding his head, not understanding much of it, ill at ease in the role of indulgent confessor. He thought he understood one thing at least after Momo declared: "Could be that I killed her, in my place anybody..." He was silent as he swallowed a gush of saliva, then added: "But the knife that was in her back, her pimp stole it off me, that I can swear. But go tell Phonse that! He could never stand me, even before I started going out with her. So he must'a thought it was too good a chance to pass up. That old bastard! If he hadn't hid himself before he shot me I could'a looked after myself."

Fred turned towards the inspector who was squeezing his arm, smiling with the corner of his lips, breathing his alcoholic breath on him: "So, Freddie boy..." He straightened up, his arm still caught in a grip that was stronger than he was used to: "According to what the wounded man said, the only guy that had any reason to shoot him was somebody called Phonse," he said without conviction, simply so as not to lose face and to feel the inspector's fingers loosen their grip.

"One thing for sure, the guy that shot him had a 30.30. Somebody that was up bright and early this morning. Just have to find out who it was. What do you think?"

Fred got to his feet and leaned on the counter, not really angry but humiliated at being treated like a child in front of the woman whose big brown eyes shone with adoration when she looked at the inspector. He tried to find a biting response, and all he could come up with was: "Where do I start?" Telling himself: "Now that's right, fall right into the trap..."

"You asking me?"

143

The inspector withdrew his hand, indifferent. "The keys," Fred asked, his hand outstretched. The inspector jangled them in his pocket before letting them drop into the hand Fred was ashamed to hold out in that manner. "You look after finding that 30.30 and don't make too much of a ruckus," the inspector concluded, not laughing, as Fred turned his back, clicking the heels of his black boots, waxed so carefully, the inspector was telling Jérôme who had arrived while all this was going on, that dogs would stop to admire their reflections. Jérôme laughed, his head thrown back, holding his belly. "You don't have to bust a gut," the inspector said, "you've laughed at that story at least twenty times," and he noticed Emérence's smile of complicity; suddenly she seemed embarrassed, asking: "Are you staying for supper?"

"All depends. If Fred gets on the track of something and it can't wait I'm afraid I'll be running all night."

"All the more reason to have a good supper," Emérence insisted; she had had time since lunch to make herself beautiful and was squeezed into a salmon-pink dress with a bodice so tight that whenever she took a deep breath her bosom threatened to leap out of its niche, which no doubt explained why the card-players downed their beer quickly, displeased when it was Jérôme who got up to serve them. The kitchen door was swinging and the aroma of roast veal with garlic wafted through the room. "An eight-pound roast," Emérence pointed out, "enough for three of us, I hope." He smiled, tearing the cellophane from his cigar, and as he was about to put his hand on Emérence's arm he heard Jérôme returning in his crepe-soled shoes: "Will you two tell me what you're plotting in there?" The inspector stuck his cigar in the corner of his mouth. "Well, if you don't mind I'm going upstairs for a nap. Wake me up for supper." Emérence gave him a broad smile covered with the softest lipstick he'd ever seen. And he went upstairs, hat in hand, chewing on the stub of his cigar. He went into the room which Emérence had perfumed and turned the arm-

chair around so he could see the lake, the bit that was still
left – a spot, almost black, in the middle of the white space.
It would be dark in a while, "not the weather for taking pictures," a dream to put off till later, until the day of his
retirement which was approaching so slowly, lingering, it
seemed to him, "just to make my life miserable." He
dropped his coat on the bed, on top of his hat. He didn't
feel like going to any trouble for such a short rest so he collapsed into the chair, put his cigar in the standing ashtray
that had been placed within his reach and closed his eyes.
"That woman could be the death of me . . . Her belly practically showing," he thought, stroking the armrests which
turned warm under his palms, then his hands were still. He
slept, mouth wide open.

He hadn't moved when, less than an hour later, she
knocked gently on the door before tiptoeing in, holding her
breath. She had lit the night-light. She was about to put her
long white hand on his bent arm: "It's no crime to watch a
man sleeping, after what Jérôme did to me," and the hesitant gesture remained suspended there, her hand stretched
out above his arm, floating, as she examined the squarish,
still young, unwrinkled face, the hair turning grey at the
temples. Her hand was still wavering, as though attracted
by the flattened hair on the skull, then she pressed on the
shoulder, which immediately shuddered. "Wake up, Paul-
Emile. Phonse wants to talk to you." He raised his arm
before opening his eyes. "What?"

"Phonse has something to tell you. Says it's urgent."

Emérence's voice had wakened him completely now. He
looked at her from under barely open eyelids. "He can't
wait, eh?" She smiled at him, forgetting her hand on his
arm. He tapped it nervously.

"Listen, Paul-Emile..."

He turned around, as though expecting some banality.
And when he deigned to look at her again her hands were
behind her back, retying the bow in her apron. "No, nothing..." He put his cigar back in the corner of his mouth and

buttoned his jacket, so worn now at the cuffs that he had got in the habit of sticking his hands in the pockets of his pants which were baggy at the knees and all creased in the back. He struck a match on his heel, lit his cigar and motioned to Emérence that he would follow her. They went downstairs, one behind the other, without a word: he sniffed the smell of cooking mingled with her perfume.

Phonse, lost in his too roomy mourning clothes, was gesticulating in front of the bar, to the silent approval of Jérôme. He rushed at the inspector, who was hiding behind the smoke of his cigar. "There you are! Takin' a snooze while your man's actin' like a bully over at Florent's. Had the nerve to ask me for the key to the house the night before the funeral; do you think that's right, Paul-Emile? And don't try and tell me you don't know nothin' about it! That clown tells me, I got orders. I'll give him orders! I ask you, is that right, searchin' somebody's house while they're down on their knees beside their own daughter's body?" The inspector shook his head, seeming moderately indignant at Fred's irreverent behaviour. "Of course not, people shouldn't behave like that. But we gotta find that goddam 30.30. Fred should'a done it different, that's for sure. If you see him, tell him I said it's suppertime. He can't ask for more than that."

Calmed down, Phonse ordered a plain gin and Jérôme served it, refusing payment, "on a day like this, eh?" and the inspector, his nose against the window pane, watched the snow drifting through the luminous orbit of the street lamp that lit the entrance to the Café Central. "Emérence had something to tell me," he thought, "if I'm not mistaken, but I pretended I didn't understand, just like I always do. Still, I'd like to know what's going on inside her head." His cigar sizzled when it touched the damp glass. Phonse went out, more bent than ever, as though to give the wind less hold. The inspector saw him go into Florent's in the patch of light that was cut off by the frame of the open door, then nothing – no light, nobody. Winter darkness. The wind scraping against the walls, carrying away the snow like an eddy. Nothing but the smell of roast veal, glasses clinking against the tables, the kitchen door swinging and creaking, and sudden bursts of laughter. Everything bored him, here or back in Terrenoire, in his dusty apartment that was paradoxically both cluttered and deserted. He thought, "It'll go away when I have something to eat."

8

Standing there for he didn't know how long – ten minutes or an hour – scowling inside the turned-up collar of his black overcoat, he looked at the coloured pictures advertising *Naked Eva*, a Swedish film that had already started, to judge from the deserted lobby. He was absolutely alone in the illuminated street, swept by a wind that carried along a fine powdery snow. His cheeks were frozen, his hands thrust into his pockets. When he left the house where he had boarded for a year, just by the Métro station, he had let himself be guided by chance, walking like a sleepwalker or an old and confused horse unable to find the road back to the stable, and he'd kept wandering through the fine snow, pushed on by the simple need to breathe, telling himself his fatigue would finally chase away all the images that kept parading through his mind, superimpositions of memories and of the pictures that had appeared on the first page of *Le Journal de Montréal* – Gigi's body covered by a blanket, forever cold, forever lost to him – and he thought that now he would be deprived of the only human flesh whose warm touch had been a source of pleasure and shame. And the poster he was staring at became confused, split, as though behind the sheets where a blonde was lying in ecstasy in the arms of a giant, naked to the waist, another one appeared to remind him that even dead, Gigi belonged to so many people's memories that there was nothing personal about

148

his own. It would just be one of those pictures, more or less successful, all printed from the same negative. He pressed his hand against the glass to keep his balance, and as he turned around he caught a glimpse of the man, curled up now, who had almost taken him with him as he fell. He put his hands on his knees and leaned over the grey-bearded face, wincing in an effort to say something. An unbearable stench of alcohol came out of the man's blue lips which opened to murmur a kind of blasphemous prayer: *"Christ de christ d'hostie"*, nothing more, just that single invocation, and then his lips began to tremble with the same convulsive trembling that was shaking the hand with the long black-rimmed fingernails. The cap did not conceal the white line of a scar that ran across the bald temple. He held out his hand, his clean, soft hand, a kind of support no one had ever used and which he doubted ever would be used. The drunk said something else, his face in the fold of his old raincoat. Saint-Pierre got up, still holding out his hand, looking around him, horrified at his own cowardice, his desire to clear out as fast as he could, but as he turned his head towards the movie-theatre, he saw the face of the cashier inside her glass cage, and it seemed to him that her eyes were judging him and condemning, no matter what he did now. Furiously he grabbed the drunk under the arm with difficulty, stood him up, almost sliding down with him; then he put his arm around the man's waist and dragged him to the delicatessen, which was so brightly lit inside that he blinked, a blush of shame pricking at his cheeks. He helped the drunk sit down in the first booth he glimpsed through his cloudy vision of the almost empty room, went to the cash register where the Greek seemed to be sizing up the situation, and offered him a dollar bill. "Give him something hot," then extracting another bill from his wallet he added, looking down, "A package of Players, please." The Greek tossed the package onto the counter and gave him his change. Saint-Pierre picked up the package as he consulted the clock that advertised Pepsi and walked back

149

to the drunk who was stretched out full-length on the bench. He squeezed his arm so hard that the man opened his eyes. And after showing him the package of cigarettes which he placed on the table he let go of him, listening to him grumble.

Outside, Saint-Pierre took a deep breath of the damp air, rubbing his hands on his overcoat, telling himself immediately: "That's me, all right, afraid to get my hands dirty," and stuck them into his pockets. He hurried back down Saint-Laurent, the wind at his back, as though he were expected somewhere, but there was only one place in the world where he could take refuge: his room littered with textbooks, exercises to be corrected and various souvenirs, most of them of maternal origin, certain he would never again go to the Paradise for a drink and wait for one of the heavily made-up women to approach him with a smile, with the obvious intention of squeezing as much money out of him as possible, "no, that's over, and besides if I'd thought about it I would have called Mademoiselle Langlais, maybe she's a bit of an old maid, but at least with her there's no danger of anything but academic contacts, and I've had enough of that!" He waved his arm as though wanting to erase from the map the stretch of street that led to the raw-yellow blinking sign of the Paradise, the billboard announcing a brand-new show, the Geishas of the Rising Sun. He had barely stopped in front of it, just out of curiosity, he thought, when the doorman appeared, a mechanism set in motion by his mere presence, and opened the door to let him in, heart pounding, blood frozen, like every other time he had risked crossing the threshold of "that den of vice," as he had described the first nightclub he dared set foot in, long before he left the seminary. He followed the inevitable short, broad-shouldered Italian who had taken his hat and coat and was overdoing his bows and smiles of complicity; meanwhile he held out a square hand which even in the half-light could judge the size of the tip that was placed there, and when it was a bill he was quick to add, "Someone will be here right away, Monsieur," and the waiter always appeared promptly.

He took a deep breath, trying to relax a little, but the orchestra was getting on his nerves. The waiter seemed embarrassed at having slapped Marlene's behind in his presence, and stood in front of Saint-Pierre, silent and distant, waiting for him to order something, "a cognac." He went away without asking which brand, holding his tray along his thigh. Saint-Pierre told himself, "After this drink I'm getting out of here." Alone at her table, Marlene was picking her fingernails; then, taking his look for an invitation, she got up and came to sit at his table, nonchalant, her mouth soft, eyes damp, wanting so obviously to please that he refrained from telling her that he could do without her services, thinking of Gigi, so different, content just to be there, full of animal presence, Gigi who didn't have to put on airs to become indispensable. Just seeing her, withdrawn into her slow sensual reverie, you needed her, you couldn't understand how you could have lived before you found yourself in the zone of peaceful warmth that she gave off. "A gimlet for me," Marlene told the glacial waiter who was placing the glass of cognac in front of Saint-Pierre. He started as he realized the waiter was still there, and slipped a two-dollar bill into his hand. Marlene had lit a cigarette and was smoking it nervously, her cheeks hollow as though the filter were clogged. "All alone now, eh?" But he didn't catch the allusion to the event which he thought about constantly. "Didn't you hear? Funny, it was in all the papers. As you can see, your Gigi isn't here. She got herself done in by a crazy. Don't tell me you didn't hear about it?"

"Ah!"

"Sometimes I get the feeling you're off in the clouds. I tell you that Gigi's dead and you just sit there staring at me. That reminds me: Nico wanted to see you."

He opened his mouth, too astounded to say anything but: "Me? Why?" He couldn't catch his breath, and he felt as though he were smothering. "I don't know," Marlene replied. "To get some details. You were at her place the night it happened. The cops came yesterday. They nearly put everybody away, even the customers."

"You're kidding!"

He forced himself to stare at his glass, suddenly feeling that he was in a trap, tracked, threatened with death because of what he knew, indifferent now to the lights, to the MC's brassy voice, to Marlene herself who had turned her back and was distributing kisses to the customers who were coming to sit at a neighbouring table. The music was slow, insidious, while three Japanese girls modestly wrapped in their silky kimonos appeared on the stage, bent over in a long bow, showing their black hair tied into a bulging chignon that looked almost blue under the lights. Then the orchestra made them turn around, the first copying the third, while the one in the middle went in the opposite direction to her partners, so fast you could barely see their eyes, made enormous by the oval of their makeup – a dazzling whirlwind of colours and pale hands that stopped without warning, turned into a slow undulation of shoulders and thighs, hands crossed on their breasts, and he thought: "If I go on like this they're going to think I've got a good reason and then..."; he saw Gigi under her blanket on the front page of the paper, below the big black headline announcing CALL GIRL VICTIM OF KNIFE-WIELDING MAD-MAN, and although the words were terrifying, they would be forgotten, erased by others just as huge and terrible, "because life goes on, it has to, and if we stopped at every news item we'd never get through...Things like that happen every day; I don't even pay attention to them." And with a violent attempt at concentration, he watched the kimonos opening, the fine legs, the round thighs, the naked hips with a black lace holding in place a G-string so small the tuft of hair was not completely hidden. They danced on their kimonos as lightly as leaves, and their pointed breasts did not quiver any more than their bellies or their cheeks. His hands were freezing; only the nerves on the surface of the skin gave him an impression of life. He held them on his thighs to warm them, squinting to the left where he could hear a stifled laugh, Frenchy's laugh, he could have sworn, but there was no way to be sure without turning his head. And then he would be forced to deal with the problem although he felt weak just at the thought of finding himself cornered there. He drank his cognac in one gulp, had one last quick look at the three dancers, kneeling now, their legs apart, arms raised, and made his way towards the toilet, followed by the whistles of the people he was disturbing. Inside the bathroom he wondered whether he'd been followed; he wanted to urinate but couldn't and he wiped his hands on the towel after doing up his zipper. The door closed behind him slowly, with the sound of a tire losing air, while he walked along the wall that led to the cloakroom. He sighed when he noticed a young girl whose face told him nothing; he handed her his ticket. She held out his coat and he tiptoed out, forgetting his hat, not saying goodnight to the doorman who was amazed to see him leave in the middle of the show. The street seemed enormous, a reassuring symbol of freedom where he felt he was not walking but swimming, carried away on the white sea of snow, so relieved that as he got farther away from the danger he had brushed against a few moments earlier he believed he was escaping from a nightmare, the hallucinating memory of Gigi's picture summarizing and concluding a night of hatred and blood in which he, too, had played a role. "Before then I was always out of the game, couldn't do badly any more than I could do well – just there, waiting for something to happen, not even sure I could get anything out of it." He moved off to the right, slowing down now that he was approaching the house, the only possible refuge against everything he had brought down on himself because he had once given twenty dollars to "that Mary Magdalene who I treated worse than a dog, and who was finally degraded because of me," he was thinking when the abrupt sound of squealing tires wrenched at his guts. He ran into the dark alley, tripping over lumps of ice and bags of garbage which burst, releasing their foul smells into his nose until he thought, panic-stricken: "Running won't help, they'll be waiting for me at the other end." Paralyzed for a moment by the certainty of his fate he crouched down as though to listen to the sounds carried on the wind, his fist closed on the cut that was burning the palm of his hand; then with a leap he retraced his steps, neck outstretched taking long strides and wondering: "What am I going to say to them if they catch me? That I was scared? And why?" He stopped before what looked like the back of a shop or restaurant. The fence had been knocked down and was almost completely buried under the snow. He opened the door, with its windows and grille, and was blinded by the light from a powerful bulb without a shade, screwed to the ceiling in the hallway that led to a locked door. "A real rat-trap," he thought, ready for anything now, feeling lost, squeezed into this cul-de-sac. I've got time before they find me..." But he knew very well that it was a poor consolation, the kind of comfort one gives oneself to stay in control of a situation. He fiddled with the thirty dollars still left in his pocket, telling himself that a stick would have been more useful, "a stick, anything, a bottle, a knife, a hammer," but immediately he saw blood pouring down his face and shook his head: "No, mustn't have that."

He leaned against the brick wall, then slid down to the wooden floor, his long legs trembling with fatigue, leaning against the door to block it, not knowing what purpose this resistance might serve, but it was all the same to him. He was cold. It was the only thing he was struggling against, remembering everything, from the first time he'd followed Gigi to her room after drinking with her for most of the evening, at the end of November, and of her complete indifference to him, while he had expected so much from her, first of all that she turn her back to put him at ease; but no, she threw clothing left and right, going back and forth in front of him, exactly as though he weren't there – her way

154

of showing her contempt for everyone who might use her like some kind of object. She watched him play with his hat, a thirty-eight-year-old man still ignorant of his own flesh, who didn't dare ask her to turn around for a few seconds to make it easier for him and was trying to tell her he'd pay her for an hour of simple conversation if she didn't feel like it – that unnamable thing which had tormented him until it drove him to this unbearable wordless promiscuity. She shrugged her shoulders, still distant, and he turned around as though getting ready to leave, but she came over to him: "Come on, you aren't gonna pull that one on me. We've wasted enough time already."

"I just don't want you to feel you have to."

His throat knotted and he was trying to talk when he was abruptly interrupted by the slamming of the bathroom door; he thought that out of modesty she would get undressed in there, perfume herself, then put on a filmy negligée, black probably, like the ones he'd seen in men's magazines and dirty movies, but all that time instead of taking advantage of her absence to relax, he examined the smallest details of the room – the lamp on the bedside table that gave off a feeble light, the knick-knacks on the chest of drawers among the jars and pencils and brushes, the whole panoply that helped make people look avidly at her – interested only in taking, in touching (so he thought as he felt the heat rise to his face), not even trying to understand or to see anything in her except an opportunity for pleasure. And when she came back stark naked, so naked he didn't feel anything, not even the paralyzing cold that had always prevented him from following that kind of woman to her room, he looked away and finally hung his hat on the door knob and took off his coat, cold sweat pouring from his armpits. "Turn off the light, as long as you're standin' there," she said, lying down on the bed, holding a tabloid paper in front of her, turned towards the lamp that shed its feeble light half on the pillow, half on the floor. And as he was stepping out of his trousers he heard the crumpling of

155

the paper, but without looking at what she was doing he guessed she was sizing him up before he could give her any proof of his virility. Then, as though fascinated by the collection of strange objects on top of the dresser, he unbuttoned his shirt with awkward, trembling fingers, came over to the bed still wearing his shoes, burning as he came close to her, throat dry, vision blurred as though the effects of the alcohol had been delayed. "I was waiting for the machine to start up without having to manipulate it," he remembered. And he heard her say, in a voice that was filtered through the thickness of the paper, "There's soap and a towel in the bathroom." He got up, even more confused, more muddled, almost staggering as he went to the bathroom where a soft cotton towel was folded over the back of the sink. The cold water numbed, then revived him. He went back into the room and she was cutting her toenails. He lay down, staring at the ceiling, not seeming to know what he was doing there. She sighed, put the scissors on the bedside table and said, almost absent-mindedly: "Do I have to take your pants off too, you big baby?" She did so, carelessly but not brusquely, maternally in a way, "yes, and I didn't even move, I was clumsier than ever"; then he felt her warm breath, a damp caress around his erect sex which seemed monstrous to him, as though it had some kind of independence since escaping from him to get lost between strange hands, lips so unfamiliar that their touch seemed some kind of invention, possibly a new kind of human species unknown until then. The feeling of absolute well-being, demanding complete immobility, had gone away, replaced by the irrepressible need to get rid of the tension that was stiffening his entire body. And as he was closing his eyes he heard a slurred, distant voice: "If you want me to smoke it right down to the butt it's five bucks extra, okay?" He made no reply, for fear that if he opened his mouth he would have to do something and that it would put an end to the warm and unexpected caress. He just held his hand out to her, and she came closer to start smoking again, as she said in her professional jargon, harder now, so that it was his very life she was sucking on while he panted, unable to hold back any longer the plaintive sounds which shamed him as they became increasingly jerky and the wave mounted inside him, blinding him, suddenly exploding between his legs.

He opened his eyes, noticed his feet against the door, the brick wall and the bare bulb, a brutal return to a world where he had to spend the night with his fear, the cold and the memory of that first physical ordeal which had not been followed by the conversation he had promised to have with the woman bending over him, her mouth full of him, disgusted with him, he was sure, a woman he had not even held in his arms. Immediately afterwards, seeing her heading for the bathroom, he got dressed feverishly, not taking the trouble to button his shirt, then he put three ten-dollar bills on the dresser and left, abandoning her to silence, to the hollow that would exist between his departure and the arrival of the next customer with whom she would start the same game. He must have walked for a good hour, going back and forth past the house where he lived a lonely bachelor's life, hoping to exhaust his remaining energy and resistance to sleep. Next morning he avoided looking at his students, replying drily to Evelyn who had stayed in the classroom after the others left to ask him where to find the documentation she needed to finish her assignment. He looked down at her briefcase as he said: "In the library, I imagine," and went out, taking long strides, leaving her stranded there. There had been a respite, two weeks of relative indifference, before desire surfaced again, aroused by Evelyn's crossed legs as she sat across from him, her skirt deliberately pulled up, smiling at him when she saw his eyes focussing on her long brown thighs. He had come to the heart of it: Evelyn or Gigi. And that Friday, walking down Saint-Laurent, he thought he had been delivered from the dream of warmth buried between Evelyn's thighs, although the worst still had to be accomplished – to pay for

Gigi's drinks as she sat there silent and aloof, then follow her and get undressed in front of her, so at ease in her own skin he wondered if he belonged to some other species. But this time he didn't bother to inspect the room, he behaved like anybody else, he thought; and when he lay down beside her he was completely composed, perhaps because she turned her back to him, something that astonished, then delighted him, preventing a painful face-to-face encounter. In any event, he allowed himself the luxury of certain fantasies, caressing her buttocks and shoulders, even sinking his face between her thighs and then, awkwardly, three times, he tried to slip inside her. She had to guide him, sighing with annoyance. She began to squirm, a regular back-and-forth movement, while he, caught there, let her go on, clutching her hips in his hands. His pleasure came very quickly, almost in a single rush that made him roar like a wounded animal. He withdrew as quickly as the first time, repeated the same blind motions – the money on the dresser, his coat over his arm, his hat on his head – and said in a very low voice: "Good night." But she just lay there, inanimate and vanquished, or so it seemed to him as he went down the stairs, anxious to be walking in the cold which not only brought him back to himself but purified him of the inhumanity he thought he would pay for one day or another by prostituting himself in turn, "do whatever some strange woman asks me, everything that is most repugnant – and why not, if I expect it from a woman?" And he envisioned his landlady, Madame Pétrie, separated from her husband for years, holding out a dollar, smiling to see him finally prepared to put up with all her whims. But he couldn't imagine her naked without immediately putting her bathrobe on her back. "Not with her, oh no!" And the day after the next he went back to the Paradise where in return for a few drinks he obtained Gigi's telephone number. Around nine o'clock he had gone to her room, a bottle of rye in his pocket: that famous night he saw Momo lying on the bed, a cigarette in his mouth, not at all intimidated by a third person so scandalously out of place. His timidity prevented him from apologizing and going away – and something else too: the need to intrude on them, burden them with his awkward presence. They deserved it, since he'd bought a bottle of rye and gone there for nothing, just to feel a total stranger's insistent look cutting through him. His malaise inspired some brand-new actions, like taking the bottle out of his pocket and saying: "We can have a drink at least?" Or sitting on the edge of the bed, rather stiff, but with a certain familiarity. Momo smiled, without saying a word. Gigi paced the floor in the room, half bedroom, half living-room, and then suggested they play poker, already shuffling the cards so fast she seemed to be shaking one hand inside the other. They played quietly, like old friends with nothing more to say to one another, at least until she got up and came back with a spray can which she aimed at Momo, spraying him with perfume, and he, amused at first, then increasingly annoyed, twisted her arm sharply. Then came the name-calling; he barely remembered getting up to intervene, not so much to fix things between them as to avoid a scene where he would be caught off guard. He went over to them, saying something – nothing especially provocative – not expecting the punch in the nose that was hard enough to stun him. Then, before he even realized what had happened, he heard Momo telling him to get lost, throwing his coat at him, as though Momo had some rights to Gigi's person that he didn't share. He went down the stairs, his legs like rubber, still suffering from the double effect of the rye and the blow.

Something moved outside. Instinctively, he pressed his feet against the door, his muscles so tense that his calves hurt, remembering that as he was coming out of the building a familiar face had appeared, framed by the door of a car parked on an angle, one wheel on the sidewalk. "Were you up there?" Frenchy asked him. "Everything all right?" His broad simian face, disfigured by a forced smile, had frightened him, but not enough to stop him from replying, in a voice that was not completely his own: "There was a bit of a family fight while I was there." The other man frowned. "And I was the one that got hit," Saint-Pierre added. Frenchy growled, his way of letting him know it wouldn't happen again. He had continued on his way, his mind empty, concerned only with putting one foot in front of the other without slipping on the packed snow. "And I'm willing to bet he's had a hand in this business," he thought. "Anyway, if Nico wanted to see me it must have been to warn me to keep quiet." He bent a leg, already stiff, suddenly anxious to get up, go out and face the blows and get it over with. "And tough luck for me that I had to be stupid enought to stick my nose in it." He got up, still trembling, and leaned against the wall, looking at the elongated shadow of his torso in the snow-filled courtyard, saying to himself: "Can't go on being scared like this. I can't drag along much longer." He felt the cold penetrating right to his bones, so cold he preferred to risk everything rather than stay there motionless, holding back the trembling of his muscles. He took a few steps towards the alley, towards the luminous cluster of street-lamps, running blindly, his arms held out before him as though he were expecting to fall.

Madame Pétrie was dozing on the sofa in front of the blue television screen. She started when she heard him cross the living room. "Ah, it's you! A fine time to be coming home! You're going to ruin your health." It was her inevitable reproach whenever he came in after midnight and she had fallen asleep during the first film of the evening. "One of these days..." she added, not finishing her sentence, stretching languorously, "nothing on under her dressing-gown," he noted. "If you'd like a hot drink don't make too much noise, M'sieu Provencher's a light sleeper." He nodded agreement, anxious to shut himself inside his room, which smelled of what? Neither tobacco nor perfume: a vague odour, an emanation of solitude permeating the sofa-bed, the drapes, the most insignificant object placed on the varnished shelves that were held up by huge blocks of grey

160

stone, "an old bachelor's smell," he thought, "as recognizable as Madame Pétrie's cooking smells or the resin smell in Gigi's apartment." He plugged in the hotplate and placed on it the pot full of coffee which he had been in too much of a hurry to drink that morning. He thought he heard his landlady's door closing and he lay down without fear of seeing her come in unexpectedly, as she sometimes did. He slipped his feet under the cushion, toes tingling. He told himself he'd never show his face at the Paradise again, at least not until this whole business was forgotten and he'd paid his debt in the arms of Madame Pétrie, who would come to look for him one of these nights when Monsieur Provencher went to the hospital to sit up with his wife. He would no longer avoid her questioning, canine look. He'd even invite her in to listen to some music – a Vivaldi concerto she kept asking him to play for her – and he'd let her do as she wished, or rather, he would do everything for her, without expecting anything in return, no pleasure, except, no doubt, that of sharing a common humiliation with Gigi. "But that can wait... For the moment..." He got up to take the pot off the burner, as the coffee had started to boil. He poured some into the china cup, imported from England, which his mother had given him though it was part of the set of dishes that had been her finest wedding present. He remembered her pained look when he left the seminary and she made up a kind of bachelor's trousseau for him – a small woman, always well dressed, all grey now in the eternal black suit which she wore even to entertain him; and she seemed to pay more attention to Zouzou's whims than to the rest of the world. "She talks chihuahua all the time. No wonder she can't think of anything to say when I take the trouble to call her or go and visit," he thought, staring at the hotplate which had been part of her maternal trousseau, along with the household objects scattered over the room. He drank his coffee without sugar or milk, just as it was, thick, black and bitter. Then he opened the door: a night-light shed a feeble glow on the part of the living-room where the squat black instrument sat that was still foreign to him, though he had used it a few times to send news to his mother in Trois-Rivières, "the only place in the world where she thinks she can breathe," he thought, putting his hand hesitantly on the telephone. He dialed a number and in a low voice asked for the police, had to repeat what he wanted, his throat tight and dry with fear, his hand shaking so badly he had trouble holding the receiver against his ear, and all he could hear was the groaning that had come from the bathroom that night at Gigi's, before Momo got up to close the door. A voice sounded in his ear, incomprehensible. He hung up, clutching the telephone as though that could ensure its silence, then, exhausted, went back to his room – so narrow and cluttered it was hard to take more than three or four steps without bumping into something. He put some cognac into his coffee and drank it down in one gulp, then poured more cognac, straight this time. He was beginning to feel warm. Then he tipped back his head – a slight inclination – and the warmth went right through him.

He unbuttoned his shirt and was warm now and completely calm, sitting on the edge of the sofa, too stupefied to concentrate on anything at all. "A nice shower will help me get to sleep," he thought, getting up; then he took such a long step that he found himself in front of the door again. Madame Pétrie was just coming out of the kitchen, holding a glass of water. "I'm going to have to take a pill if I want to get any sleep."

"I'm the same way."

He wondered if it was his tone of voice or his haggard appearance that embarrassed her, made her hesitant and confused, her eyes shifting from the glass of water to the unbuttoned shirt, open on his chest covered with black hair. "If she knew I've got hair like that even on my back..." he thought, already sitting in the armchair to the right of the sofa, while she set her glass on the low table in the middle of the carpet, then got up again, her hand on her chest as though to slow down the beating of her heart: "We can wait up a bit. But come over here and sit with me." And he got up, rather abruptly, with a short nervous laugh.

9

Dulled by the breakfast he'd just eaten, the inspector had not opened the paper bag full of fudge Emérence had made especially for him – it was their farewell ritual, the last word in a meeting not marked by much conversation. Jérôme had offered him a long cigar and they were having their first smoke of the day, sitting at the table where Emérence had just put down the coffee-pot. "Great," the inspector said, taking the cigar out of his mouth as though to submit it to a minute examination. "Anything new?" Jérôme asked, but the inspector kept staring at his cigar, seeming upset. "Nothing new...Imagine how I slept last night. But I'm not leaving here alone, that I can guarantee! Let people laugh behind my back because I couldn't find the sneaky bastard that wanted to take justice into his own hands. Not on your life!" Jérôme was twiddling his thumbs, nodding his head which was made less round by his wavy wig, "looks like an egg," the inspector thought, suddenly feeling an urge to make fun of him. "Listen, Jérôme, if I was you I wouldn't bother. Everybody's always seen you with your skull as bare as your bum," but he didn't open his mouth, only smiled, turned towards Emérence, on his left: "Anyway, you fed me well, Emérence. I feel as though my liver's as big as a melon, and it's a wonder it isn't." She brought her hand to her throat, letting out a long sigh. "Well, it's your own fault if you don't take advantage of it longer. Why don't you come and use our place more often?"

"You'd be singing another tune if I did, because I'd really like to move in somewhere around here next summer."

Emérence looked at him, her fine brown eyes lowered, a faint hint of a smile lengthening her lips, while Jérôme patted his back: "Best news I've heard in a long time, Paul-Emile! That way we won't miss you so much. Or if we do we won't be alone." And he burst into his belly laugh which spread through him as though it were inside a huge sounding-box. "Watch out for the windows," the inspector said laconically, his hat on the back of his head, already putting on his tweed coat, "And thanks for the fudge, Emérence, just in case I don't come back this way after Mass. I left an envelope on the bed."

"Come on, you didn't have to do that!" she protested.

"My expenses are paid."

But Jérôme was no longer laughing; he turned pale as he stared at her with eyes like nearly transparent marbles, neither blue nor grey. "You're acting like a total stranger," she insisted.

"Everybody's got to live," the inspector said as he backed toward the door.

"That's true," Jérôme cut in, very philosophical, already reassured by his guest's imminent departure.

And as soon as the door was closed he looked her up and down, his forefinger stuck in the artificial mop of his right sideburn: "What's got into you? One of the few customers we've had in the last month and you tell him he doesn't have to pay!" She almost answered something, but kept it to herself, leaped to her feet, holding the coffee-pot and ran with heels clattering to take refuge in the kitchen while he went on preaching at her: "I know you'd give him the moon. He brings you presents but what does he do for me, eh? Besides, I give him cigars and he hardly even takes the trouble to say thanks." But she heard nothing, deafened by

165

the water roaring out of the tap.

Fred was soaking toast dripping with butter in his egg yolk, so sleepy he seemed not to recognize the inspector who was standing in front of him, hands folded across his belly. "Have a good night?"

"Ah, it's you! I was just having a bite to eat."

"That's what I figured you were doing."

"Didn't have any luck," and wiped his mouth with the stained paper napkin on which he had placed his knife. "Didn't find anything."

"Do you mind telling me where you were? We waited all night for you."

Fred leaned against the back of the booth, just long enough to retrace the thread of the events or find a reply that would be plausible enough not to make the inspector laugh: "Well, a funny thing happened. So to speak, because you'll never guess what...I fell asleep in the Buick after I'd had a coffee with the waitress, what's her name?"

"You mean you spent the whole night in the Buick?"

"No, not the whole night. I don't know what time it was when I woke up. Six o'clock, seven maybe."

"And what did she have to say?"

He finally sat down across from Fred, arms folded, leaning against the back of the booth, his eyes nearly closed as though he were listening to the gentle crackling of the glowing tip of his cigar. Fred blushed as he bent down to pick up the knife he had dropped, speaking in a muffled voice, his neck squeezed into the tight collar of his khaki-coloured shirt: "That girl, I forget her name, just try and make her talk. But what she didn't know, I was already pretty close when the other guy, her fiancé, showed up. At one point I heard him say, loud enough so everybody could hear, that it wasn't him that had shot at Momo, but it pissed him off because he wouldn't'a missed. It wouldn't'a been one bullet but two, three, maybe even more, he would'a drilled into Momo. I don't think the girl liked that very much. Anyhow, I saw her take off as fast as a golf ball."

166

"You look tired, Fred. Know what you should do? Go and get a breath of air. Twenty minutes from now, half an hour, let's say, you come and meet me at Lavallée's place; you remember where it is, I hope?"

Fred stared fixedly at his hands spread out on the table, as though astonished at their uselessness, shaking his head: "So I'm gonna be sitting around with nothing to do, as usual?"

"What do you mean, nothing to do? Just because I tell you to take a little walk and come and meet me in twenty, twenty-five minutes? You hard of hearing, Fred?"

He sighed, unable to argue any longer, and even if he'd wanted to it would have been a waste of energy because the inspector had already gone, his hat stuck on his head at an angle. Fred saw him stop to buy cigars, slip them into his jacket pocket and disappear behind the door, apparently indifferent to the look that was discharging a machine gun in his back.

The sky was bright, streaked with fine powdery lines, and the inspector sniffed at the brisk air, saying to himself: "If we don't have any evidence we're going to have to resort to a bit of hanky-panky and I'm not too crazy about that." Wearing their scarecrow suits, people were on their way to the church where the funeral service was about to start. He ran into Louis-Joseph and was struck by the resemblance to Calixa and Momo, "the same thin lips, same tobacco-leaf skin, same coal-black eyes that look at you without seeing," seeing Momo again lying in the snow, his huge astonished eyes, his jaw snapping at the air like a fish and his lip so swollen he seemed to be afflicted with a harelip. "Maybe you're the one that killed her, but that's no reason," he thought as he stood in front of the church, watching the people going in, shaking the snow off their feet. Then he went over to the bakery. You couldn't go any farther; the road ended there. Behind it was the woods, then nothing. He went into the bushes which clung to his overcoat and broke with a crackling sound. The ground dropped off,

167

forcing him to slow down. "The river," he thought, and took the risk of crossing it, walking cautiously, holding out his arms on either side of him, feet apart, ready to leap. But the stream was frozen. "Good, there we are!" and he came up to the row of houses across from the church, located the store, recognizable by a sort of shed covered with corrugated tin. The door opened when he pushed it. Cardboard boxes, cases of beer and soft drinks piled up to the ceiling. He had to try a dozen keys before he opened the door that led into the kitchen. The table hadn't been cleared; there were still two bowls with milk-soaked cereal in the bottom. The quart of milk stood in the middle of the table. He went up the stairs to the bedrooms. He couldn't help it, the stairs creaked, although he took the precaution of leaning on the bannister. The first room, darkened by a seamed, yellowed window-blind, must be Joseph's, judging by the brown, crudely retouched photographs in their broad gilt frames, the big brass bed still unmade and the strong smell of tobacco. He opened the closet door – nothing but trousers with their suspenders and faded shirts. He crossed the hallway to find the same disorder in a room that was even smaller but better lighted. Tall black boots with high heels were standing under a chair covered with a stack of clothes. "Never seen boots like that around here. Phil must play Zorro in his off hours," he thought; "all he'd need is the 30.-30." And opening the closet door partway he saw a lined leather jacket, the belt dangling. "His uniform, I suppose," and took down the hanger, which felt heavy. One of the pockets was filled with long, tapered bullets. He rolled some of them in the hollow of his hand. The lead was cold. He replaced the hanger on the broom handle which served as a rod and went back downstairs, unconcerned about whether the stairs creaked or not.

No sound except his own breathing alternating with the slight crackling of his cigar, but he felt he was being spied on, even if the only real danger was that of being seen from outside. Bent double, he ran to the door of the cold-room and lifted the iron bar. The air seemed to weigh down on him immediately, as though animal flesh had fed on it until nothing was left but a cloying smell of raw meat. He hesitated before the legs of pork, the quarters of beef and the long chains of sausages. The cold was clutching at his knuckles and knees. He staggered, his stomach upset by the suffocating smell of flesh and fat. And he went out of the room, leaving behind him the incongruous odour of his cigar, "too late for that, but I couldn't take any more," he thought, indignant and furious at having had to confront the indecent and brutal display, and for nothing. He lingered for a long moment, his back against the door. Then: "What am I waiting for? For the 30.30 to fall into my hands or for somebody to catch me with my face hanging out?" As he was bending over again to go back to the kitchen a shadow crossed one of the windows. Fred had parked in front of the store. He's overdoing it," the inspector thought; "I tell him twenty minutes and here he is ready to break down the door if I don't get there on time." He went out without locking the door, walked around the store, even at the risk of being seen, and came up behind Fred, his nose pressed against the window. "Don't wear your eyes out, Fred." Fred turned around so fast he nearly knocked the inspector over, and before he had even recovered from his surprise: "Go hide on the concession road up there, behind the ranch. Stay there till I give you the sign to come down." Fred turned up the collar of his Khaki coat, as silent as though the wind had taken the words from his mouth, and the inspector saw him go, very stiff, get into the Buick, start it abruptly, skid a little and stop at the intersection of the back road. "You call that hiding!" He had a bad taste in his mouth. He spat out his cigar, no longer than a cork now, and waited in vain for the usual sizzling sound, like when you put a wet glove on the stove. "The snow's too dry," he said, attracted by the *De profundis* he could hear from the church now that someone had opened the door. Bertha's voice dominated the choir whose Laurentian accent had lost none of its rusticity. He cleared his throat and spat between his feet on the floor of the gallery. The spittle froze in the cold.

Ti-Pit came out of the church. In another few seconds he'd have been on the road without noticing the inspector leaning against the brick-paper wall of the general store. As soon as the inspector realized he'd been discovered he pretended to be interested in the distended stitches through which he could see the skin of his right thumb, but it was too late. Ti-Pit was coming closer, "no bigger than a dwarf," he thought; and in fact the postman was considered to be the smallest man in the county, so small that sometimes after a storm they couldn't see him coming along the road. "I got something to tell you," he began, when he had reached the inspector's chin; the latter changed his posture, trying to shrink down as much as he could, ashamed to seem to be crushing under his height a man who had often helped him out just by opening his mouth. "You'd like to know how much I get out of the government, eh Pit?" The postman, muffled up to the bottom of his ears, stared at him as though he had really never dared to ask himself such a question. His eyes blinked behind the softened visor of his blue cap. "It's serious, Inspector, what I got to tell you. But on the other hand, I wouldn't want you to think I wanted to hurt somebody I've known all my life."

"So what did you find out, eh?"

But Ti-Pit was smiling maliciously, indifferent to any reference to his mania for peddling gossip, rumours or scandal-mongering, as though he were certain he'd come into the world to serve as spokesman for each and everyone. Nothing could hold him back, not even the risk of arousing long-lasting hatreds – and he had quite a few to his credit – from transmitting to the first person who happened along whatever slander was making the rounds. He had always accepted his role, knowing very well that people sometimes used him, to the detriment of the truth. He would begin by scratching his forehead or shaking his head, then he would speak. This time he rubbed his hands after blowing in them and slipping them inside leather mittens of that bright yellow colour used by the Roads Department. "Well, this morning Germaine told me to come over, and she told me to tell you that early that morning Momo got killed..." The inspector started: "What do you mean, killed? He wasn't killed!"

"Well, we hadn't heard nothing about him, so we were starting to think maybe he'd popped off all of a sudden. But gettin' back to Germaine, she told me out in front of the church just before Mass that she'd seen Jos running back behind the store and he was carryin' somethin' under his arms; search me what it was, I don't know."

"Thanks anyway, but how come Germaine didn't tell me herself what she thinks she saw?"

"Well, put yourself in her place! Jos's lived next door all his life and besides her husband's in politics, you must'a..."

"Okay, thanks again," the inspector interrupted, not wanting to hear anything about local municipal politics.

Ti-Pit gave him a military salute before going off towards the bakery. "As long as I've got time to act before the news makes the rounds of the village...I can't just tell him point blank, somebody saw you that morning with something that might have looked like a rifle. On the other hand, if I take too many detours I'm going to be left dangling," and without thinking about it, with a gesture that had become automatic, his hand went inside his coat, took a cigar out of his jacket pocket and stuck it in the corner of his mouth.

People were coming out of the church. The coffin, carried by Phonse, Florent and his two sons, was escorted by the rest of the village. The inspector put the still intact cigar back in his pocket and rummaged through his coat in search of the bag of fudge. He was nibbling at a piece as he approached the general store; Phil was trying to open the door, apparently with the wrong key. The inspector waited for him to go in, then looked through the window with its

171

thick coating of frost which had an odour as pungent as dust breathed in from too close. Phil hung up his coat, took off his hat and tied behind his back the strings of his apron which was spotted at stomach level. The inspector went in, his hand on his hat. "How's things, Phil?"

"I'm just back from Mass," he said in his slow, deep voice, similar, the inspector thought, to the voice a cow would have if it were given the gift of speech.

They stared at one another, both of them caught off guard, with nothing more to say to each other. Leaning on the counter, the inspector asked: "Is Marie-Rose any better?"

"Must be," Phil replied, sulky. He added, after running some water over his hands: "The *curé* made Phonse bawl this morning with his stories about Sodom and I don't know what all. It was as if he wanted to send Gigi straight to Hell. But she isn't the worst one in this whole business. Momo isn't just a thief. He killed her! But that didn't seem to be bothering the priest. Just because Gigi made her money with Satan he figured he had to get his digs in. Good thing he commended her soul before he was through, otherwise I know one person that wouldn't be none too happy."

Then he was silent, tired after saying so much. The inspector savoured the fudge melting in his mouth, thinking it would be better if he just left everything and went back to Terrenoire. "The homicide squad's going to be losing a player before long," he thought, sitting in the rocking-chair, which he had turned around to keep an eye on Phil, busy filling his meat grinder with soft, blood-tinged chunks of beef. A door closed as he struck a match against the rocker of the chair. Then Phil plugged in the machine and ground beef came oozing out like toothpaste, slowly, then plopped into an enamel basin. It was no longer bleeding flesh but some refined product, purified of all blood, just a pinkish, rather appetizing paste. He waited for the motor to stop before saying as he leaned on the counter: "I still wonder what you were doing outside that morning Momo got a

30.30 bullet in his shoulder." He spoke with a kind of concentrated fury, as though he'd just discovered that he had been the dupe of a sinister joke. But Phil didn't flinch; he picked up the heavy basin of ground meat, holding it against his stomach, looking as though he wondered what he was going to do with it, and quickly put it away between the bowl of *cretons* and the overflowing bowl of glabrous, speckled sausages. The scraping of the bowl made a steady sound, not loud enough however to muffle the slight creaking that made him shudder and say very quickly: "I'm afraid I'm going to have to take you with me, Phil, since you're the only person who was seen outside just then. Especially because you were wandering around with a gun." Phil stopped breathing. He was staring at something behind the inspector who turned around and found himself facing Joseph pointing the 30.30 at his belly.

The inspector instinctively brought his hand up to his hat. Joseph was trembling as he held the rifle, eyes wide open and blazing with terror, as though he were anticipating the fate of the man before him, who didn't dare complete his action but simply frowned while Phil repeated for the third time: "What's got into you, Pa?" The inspector felt Phil's breath against his neck. Joseph moved back, still pointing the rifle at the inspector's chest. "Do you think I'm gonna let him get away without doin' nothin', my boy, just because he's gotta find a guilty man so he can collect his pay on Friday?" Phil was breathing hard. "I haven't accused Phil of murder yet," the inspector said, his hand on the counter. "I've got one piece of evidence against him, that's all. Just enough to take him away."

Joseph tried to laugh, but he only managed to expose the bumpy arch of his empty gums. "You policemen think you're smarter than the rest of us, eh? I don't know why I don't just drill you!" The inspector was having trouble breathing, his throat bone dry. "Drop that, Pa, he can go away by himself," Phil moaned, but Joseph wasn't even looking at him, his eyelid trembling under a big brown wart. "You need evidence to convict a man," the inspector said. "If we don't find any I'll bring Phil back to you safe and sound, that I can promise." Without too much hope he had counted on the confidence the village people had had in him since he had learned to talk like them, to appreciate their self-esteem and their crazy habits. But Joseph was laughing enthusiastically now, his gaze wandering, not directed anywhere. "You'll never have any proof it was him, never! You wanna know why?" There was a moment of silence, then: "Because that big ox there – look at him! Can't even hold onto the girl that was practically his wife. Do you think he'd ever get it into his thick skull how to get rid of a trouble-maker like Momo?" The barrel of the rifle was wandering around, dangerously unstable, between the inspector and Phil who were both frozen to the spot. "Good," said the inspector, "if you say it can't be Phil, we'll see." Joseph was laughing like a madman and stammering: "Him? Doesn't even know how to shoot. Even a cow fifteen feet away, he'd'a missed it. And you can't tell me any different, Phil. He's just good to knock off an ox with a sledge-hammer."

"Sit down now," said the inspector gently, as though he were speaking to an invalid.

Joseph was chewing on the inside of his cheek, eyelids lowered, on the verge of tears, the inspector thought as he looked at the rifle aimed at his legs. Joseph slumped into the chair, his head against the back, very erect, as though not to lose sight of the movements of the two men who were, however, motionless, listening to their own breathing alternating with the creaking of the floor under the rocking chair. "Maybe my witness made a mistake. Phil most likely spent the night at home, without going out, thinking it was natural for Marie-Rose to go to Momo's place and make him a coffee." Joseph only smiled, holding in one hand the gun which was swinging up and down, up and down, with the same slow, regular motion as the chair. And it seemed that he was now speaking only to the inspector: "They figured Jos Lavallée was sound asleep durin' all that...Always goin' around like some old bum, can't count on him for nothin'...He picked up his gun, he hid nearby in the woodshed behind the spruce trees, and he waited there a while, but then when that wild Indian showed his face, *bang, bang!*"

"You know that ain't true, Pa," Phil said, his breathing as noisy as though he were exhaling into a hollow pipe.

His father stared at him, calm now, although his voice still had its cutting edge. "Oh, so it ain't true, eh, you big ox? You'd be better off if you didn't say nothin'. Make your father do what anybody would'a done in your place. Anybody!" Phil was no longer breathing down the inspector's neck; no doubt he had lowered his head, or ceased to be alive, paralyzed forever. The inspector moved slowly behind the chair that seemed to be rocking Joseph who was leaning, very erect, against the back, and took away the 30.30, saying: "Come on now, Jos, we're going into town together," one hand on his shoulder, bony under the lining of his jacket. Jos got up, hesitating to walk, looking like a blind man without his cane. "Where's that, to town?" The inspector helped him put on the coat he had thrown onto the kitchen table when he came in. They went out rather ceremoniously, not even saying goodbye to Phil, who was prostrate on the counter, sobbing, "Don't say that, Pa, don't say that."

The dazzling snow made him close his eyes and he could have passed for a scarecrow, black and lost as he was in the streaming whiteness of the morning which was drawing to an end. His hands dangled, too white, beside his coat. The inspector whistled and gestured to Fred to come over, then he put his free hand under Jos's arm.

Fred had put the Buick behind the store, got out to question the inspector who, looking up to Heaven, had to open the back door himself. Fred got behind the wheel, waiting for his orders. "Let's go!" the inspector commanded. They started off slowly. Ti-Pit, who was coming out of the Café

Central, his mailbag by his side, watched them pass, pick up speed as soon as they had passed the Hôtel, and disappear into the turn that was considered to be the town limits. The inspector sighed, trying to understand Joseph's vague look, his eyelid trembling slightly under the big wart like the skin of a horse being tickled by a big fly. He took the paper bag out of his pocket, opened it, then offered it to Jos: "You like fudge?" Joseph nodded, or was it the lurching of the Buick that jolted him, as he sat seemingly fascinated by the posts that paraded past them on both sides of the road. "He must be thinking of his big ox bawling all by himself in the empty store." And it seemed to him that he could still hear Phil's voice, "Don't say that, Pa, don't say that."